UNDER THE RAINBOW

A novel
by
Randall Silvis

THE PERMANENT PRESS
Sag Harbor, New York 11963

Library of Congress Cataloging-in-Publication Data

Silvis, Randall, 1950–
  Under the rainbow / by Randall Silvis.
    p.   cm.
  ISBN 1-877946-28-1 : $22.00
  I. Title.
  PS3569.I47235U5   1993
  813'.54—dc20   92-34300
                                    CIP

Manufactured in the United States of America

First Edition, November 1993 -- 1600 copies

THE PERMANENT PRESS
Noyac Road
Sag Harbor, NY 11963

This book is for Rita and for Bret and for Nathan

Donald's toenails are holding him back. They are too long. There is something metaphysical about it, he thinks; about this inverse relationship between nail length and luck. He has had not a bit of good luck for over a month now. At least a month has passed since last he trimmed his nails.

Now, even as he searches the bathroom for nail clippers, he resents his accomodation of what surely is, another part of him warns, mere superstition. But that is what I am, he thinks; a superstitious man. He is made to look silly by his many superstitions, made to look neurotic, although only to himself and his wife Jessica, fortunately, for he takes great pains to conceal his superstitions in public. He knows how unreasonable they are. How indefensible.

For nearly thirty years now—maybe forty; he remembers so little of his childhood—he has been telling himself such things as, If I trim my nails my luck will change. Over the years he has trimmed his nails in excess of three hundred times, but how often have his fortunes correspondingly improved? Once? Twice?

And yet he continues to hope. Metaphysics is his last resort.

* * *

"Jess?" Donald calls from the top of the stairs. "Where did you hide the nail clippers?"

The clippers are missing from the bathroom. The medicine cabinet is virtually bare. On the top shelf lays a thermometer, on the bottom a tube of triple antibiotic salve. Donald gazes upon those vacated shelves and goes weak. There are no drugs, no medicines, no remedies anywhere inside his house. The flu season is but a few months away.

Donald's fifteen-year-old son Travis has been trying to kill himself lately. He tried aspirins but gave himself away by puking in his bedroom. He tried carbon monoxide but the car idling in the garage screwed up the television reception, so that Donald went out to the garage during a Light Days Oval Pads commercial and confiscated the car keys. Travis tried zapping himself in the left temple with the stungun from his grandmother's purse, but all he accomplished was to whack his head against the wall when he passed out, only to awaken three minutes later with a trumpeting headache. And this time there were no aspirins in the house.

Jessica has emptied the house of all medicines and cleaning solutions, any substance which by ingestion might reduce a healthy six-foot boy to a stony corpse. She has thrown out Donald's .44 revolver and his .22 automatic. She has replaced the GE gas oven with a Whirlpool electric model. She has junked every knife and pair of scissors and every vaguely bladed object she could find.

* * *

"But nail clippers?" Donald asks. "How can he possibly hurt himself with nail clippers?"

"He's very determined," she says.

"I honestly don't think he's the stabbing or slicing or clipping type."

"That's something we need never find out, do we?"

"I think he's just dabbling," says Donald. "He's fascinated by the *idea* of death. He's experimenting."

"Life isn't a chemistry set. This is dangerous."

7

"I blame it on your mother," Donald says.

Travis is not sad or depressed or morbid or morose or sullen or bellicose or brokenhearted or lonely or despondent. He is neither melancholy nor timorous. Neither dolorous nor gloomy. He is not confused about his sexuality, or, it seems, about anything else. In fact Donald wishes that *he* could be as happy as his suicidal son.

Travis is eager to die because he loves all things beautiful and he believes that death is the ultimate beauty. The consummate reward. The doorway into the finest art gallery in all creation, meditation room of the sublime, orchestra pit for the celestial musicians, heaven, the culmination, the final frontier.

Donald isn't so sure.

*   *   *

Donald would feel more comfortable talking to Travis if the boy were not so tall. Donald, at five feet ten and a half inches, feels dwarfed by his slender son. Donald sees himself as a shrinking gnome with grotesquely long toenails, dwarfed not so much by Travis's extra two inches of height as by his exuberance, his élan, his, strange as it sounds, *joie de vivre*.

"Promise me you won't try something like

this again," Donald says while holding a cold compress to the goose egg laid on Travis's skull by the stungun attempt. "Promise me that this nonsense will stop."

"I wish I could, Dad," says Travis with a dopey smile. "But sometimes I just feel so dingdonged happy, I can't help myself."

Helplessness is a condition Donald understands; too well. He has a mistress.

* * *

"Just don't ever get the idea that I am your mistress," Donald's mistress, Leeanne, chides one evening. "I am your lover, your companion, your friend, your soulmate, your confidante, your ally, your counsel, your comrade, your pal."

To Donald's eyes, she is none of these things.

"I am also," she reminds him, "vice president in charge of merchandising. The youngest vice president and the only female vice president in the history of my company. So I am nobody's fucking mistress. But you, you're not even management. You're a photographer, and a freelancer at that. You don't even have a master's degree! So if anybody here is a mistress, mister, it's you. You're mine."

"May I borrow your toenail clippers?" he asks.

* * *

Donald blames Deirdre, Jessica's mother, for Travis's current view of death. Deirdre, a widow, lives three blocks away, visits daily, showers Travis with expensive gifts, and, since before the boy could utter a word, has been schooling him in the doctrine of doom. It is a religion that should have frightened the bejeezus out of the boy, should have made him just as fearful and neurotic as the rest of western civilization. And yet, somehow, Deirdre's tutelage has backfired. Despite all the sermons Travis endures with a smile, all the pamphlets Deirdre reads to him, he has managed to absorb but a tiny percentage of her dogma.

Deirdre preaches the evil of drugs, sex, rock music, condom machines, masturbation. She prophesizes the end of the world in seven short years, the horror and unrelenting agony of Armageddon, mankind's innate wickedness, the underlying villainy of life.

Travis listens patiently, even attentively. At the end of each session he pulls her into his arms, kisses her floury cheek. "Thanks for caring so much, Grandma. You're A-number one."

Travis is a flowerchild thirty years too late.

Donald wonders if the boy's brain is producing an overabundance of L-dopa. Or if he, Donald, has somehow passed on a demented gene. If his sperm is stunted. If he is the bequeathor of a fucked-up chromosome.

"He's dyslexic or something," Deirdre says to Donald and Jessica.

Jessica says, "He gets straight A's. He's an honor student."

"He must be reading subversive literature."

"Only what you give him to read," Donald says.

"This is what happens," says Deirdre, "when a boy grows up without a strong male role model."

"Hey, what am I?" Donald asks. "I taught that boy baseball and basketball and soccer and chess. I've taken him swimming and skiing and camping and spelunking. I'm teaching him to drive. I gave him his first haircut. I taught him how to pee standing up. I have been with that boy every single day of his entire life!"

Deirdre looks severely at Donald's wife. "If you don't get that child to a doctor soon, I will."

*   *   *

When shaving, Donald always shaves from

11

the left side of his face to the right. Always buttons his shirt from the bottom to the top. Always pauses outside his son's bedroom before retiring, lays a guardian kiss upon the door, whispers too softly for anyone to hear, "Sleep tight, my darling. Daddy loves you."

Always, each time Jessica drives off to work or to the market or elsewhere, Donald stands at the window and watches her safely out of sight.

Always, whenever *he* drives off somewhere, Donald cuts a quick glance back at the house, wishes it well until his return.

Always he pisses into the left side of the toilet bowl. When using a public urinal, he makes certain to squirt into each of the drain holes, moving left to right from the bottom hole to the top.

Always, he locks every door in the car before driving his family anywhere.

Always he pulls on his left shoe first, ties the laces, then puts on the right.

All of these habits, these and the many more he performs daily, are more than mere habits to Donald. He performs them consciously, and feels somehow off-balance, incomplete, if he neglects one of them. They are tiny rituals for him, protective behaviors.

A psychologist might tell Donald that he is an obsessive personality. Donald does not care what a psychologist might say. Psychologists know absolutely nothing about the human soul, its need for rhythm, the vibrations of perfection, the frequency modulation of truth.

All Donald knows is that these little rituals of his, these neurotic habits, are important.

He does not know why.

* * *

Donald worries about his son but he does not know how to talk to him. It isn't natural to be so happy. Especially at fifteen. Maybe, as Jessica fears, such happiness *is* dangerous. Jessica's mother certainly thinks so. But Jessica's mother is dangerous.

"Travis is too big for his age," she complains. "He's bigger than anybody in our family, Jessie. Bigger than yours too, Donald."

"You don't know everybody in my family," Donald says.

"I know everybody I care to know. And a few I don't."

Donald at fifteen was a thoroughly miserable boy. And look, he thinks, how well I've turned out. Superstitious, neurotic, guilt-ridden, clinging to improbable hopes. A perfectly ordinary man. Still, Donald wants something more for his son, his only child.

"Have his hormones checked," Deirdre advises. "He acts like a neutered cat."

"His hormones are just fine," Donald says.

"How do *you* know? Have you caught him masturbating?"

Donald is too savvy to fall for this trick question. If he answers yes, Deirdre will launch into a tirade about the sins of onanism, the spiritual filth of self-abuse. She might even accuse Donald of Peeping Tomism, closet homosexuality, incestuous tendencies. If he answers no, she will attack him for taking no interest in his son, a negligent father, inferior example of a man.

Donald, for his part, wonders in silence. Is Travis's senseless happiness evidence of a kind of retardation? Up's Syndrome? Chemical imbalance? And if so, what is Donald's duty as a father? To arrange for special training? Drug therapy? Institutionalized care?

* * *

Donald wishes he had someone to talk to. Someone to talk *through*. A kind of bellhorn from whom his crowded thoughts would blos-

14

som more eloquently, more persuasively into the ears of Travis, Jessica, Deirdre, the world.

Donald once had a friend who would have served such a purpose well. Jerry, a smooth talker, a natural orator, a former lawyer, dead now, gone these many years. Not many really but enough to be quintessentially gone; four years, four-tenths of a decade. He had died at the age of forty-one, cardiac arrest while honeymooning with his fourth wife in St. Croix. He had been parasailing at the time. When they brought him down out of that blue Caribbean sky (Donald watched it again and again on the videotape Jerry's wife gave to Donald at Jerry's funeral), when they splashed him down gently in that blue Caribbean sea, everybody had thought Jerry was sleeping or faking sleep, his body limp, a dangler, he dipped into the waves so politely, a courteous man, no struggle with death.

Donald and Jerry had been buddies since their undergraduate days. College roommates. Both graduated with honors from the Communications program. Donald became a freelance photographer, hustling from one assignment to the next, never earning more than thirty thousand a year, depending on the income from his wife's flower shop to get them over the rough spots at the beginning, middle, and end of every month. Jerry went on to law school, hung out his own shingle, started his own firm, became a millionaire by the age of thirty-five, married four wives, fathered six children, engaged in (he claimed) affairs with over a hundred different women, and died without a whisper, without a single voiced regret, while gliding like an angel through a thin cerulean sky.

*   *   *

Donald has another friend, a bachelor, never married, his best friend now that Jerry has sailed out of the picture, a high school English teacher named Wright. But Wright hasn't spoken to Donald in over three months now, won't answer the door when Donald knocks, won't reminisce about Jerry over a pitcher of beer, won't do any of the things they used to do because Donald knows what Wright did not want anyone to know, that Wright is dying too, of prostate cancer, that particularly masculine way to die.

Over three months ago Donald drove to Wright's house to invite him along on an assignment, photos for the city zoo's new brochure, mug shots of the polar bears, mudwrestling hippos, spider monkeys at play. Donald arrived on Wright's block just in time to see Wright's Toyota heading down the street. Donald follows, stays out of sight, makes it a game. Wright parks beside the Medical Arts Building, goes inside and walks down the long hall of the first floor, enters a waiting room through a doorway marked UROLOGY: DRS. SEHERAN AND ARMITRAGE.

Donald hides in the hallway until the receptionist tells Wright to go into the office now, and Wright trudges into the office, and Donald takes a seat in the waiting room with his ear all but pressed to Dr. Seheran's door.

Donald hears the doctor's voice, which should be lilting and melodious with its East Indian accent, but is as flat and black and heavy as a pancake griddle. Wright's face when he emerges from the office is flat too, the griddle has walloped him but good.

Donald escorts Wright silently to his car, they scuff along side by side, Donald at one point slipping an arm around Wright's shoulder and squeezing him close. Without goodbyes, Wright climbs into his car and drives away. Donald follows; follows Wright home. But Wright refuses to answer the door when Donald knocks. Wright refuses to answer the bell, the telephone. Donald waits in ambush for him at the high school where Wright teaches, but learns that Wright has gone on extended sick leave, nobody knows why.

Donald telephones daily. He leaves a short message on Wright's answering machine. "Hey buddy, it's me again. Just wanted you to know I'm here. Whenever you're ready, just call. Don't try to go through this thing alone."

And Donald sits in the basement where his own office is. His own phone and answering machine. His darkroom. His space. He sometimes sits in the darkroom with the door locked, all lights extinguished but for the dim red bulb he uses when processing film.

Hanging on a single strand of wire suspended across the room is a strip of film, stillshots Donald made from Jerry's honeymoon videotape. The red light shines through these dangling negatives to cast Jerry dimly on the wall. Jerry hanging limp against a flat gray sky, neither rising nor falling, neither living nor dead.

Sometimes Donald talks to this shadow; he asks questions, he voices fears.

More and more often of late, Jerry answers.

* * *

Donald seeks advice, enlightenment, from

18

Mrs. Tesler, Travis's music teacher. She is a full-bodied woman, amply-fleshed, not yet forty, face as round and happy as a sunflower. They are alone in a bright room filled with instruments, golden tubas and shiny xylophones, a drum set, bass viola, piano. Pasteboard cases embracing clarinets and flutes, oboes and saxophones. Row after row of hard metal chairs. Mrs. Tesler smells of chocolate fudge, a quarter-pound block of it on the piano. Playing softly from the stereo speakers mounted on the walls are James Galway and the Tokyo Strings, a song of the sea, kelpy strands of sweetness.

Donald tries not to look too frequently at Mrs. Tesler's breasts. One fleeting glimpse every thirty seconds seems about right. He would like to dive into their softness, curl up between them, cover himself, hole-up in that bodywarm den, two bales of breathing flesh. She considers his question, innocently phrased: "How's Travis coming along?"

She sucks a crumb of chocolate from her middle finger. Donald would like to fuck her in the sound booth. "Travis is a joy," she says. "Not only is he developing into a very fine baritone, but he is . . . how can I put this? He's the most lovely young man I have ever had the pleasure to instruct."

Donald wonders what to make of this compliment. He has heard similar remarks from the neighbors of serial killers.

"In your opinion then, he's doing okay? Socially as well as academically?"

"Academically, he's at the head of his class. But you know that already. Socially, Travis is the most popular boy in school. Everybody adores him. He's gracious, polite, compassionate, considerate of every other student in the school, no matter what his or her social and/or economic status."

Donald wants to wring his hands. Oh my, oh my, what's to become of my boy?

"I'm certain he'll be elected student body president this fall," Mrs. Tesler says. "And him only a junior. It's unprecedented!"

Donald wants to thrust his head between Mrs. Tesler's all-ensconcing breasts. He wants to sob his guts out as her hand pats softly and her deep voice murmurs, "There there. There there now." He wants to fall asleep with the taste of chocolate in his mouth. He wants to sleep without dreams, hearing only the muffled pulsing of breast-blood in his ears, muted strains of Galway's flute, a fluttering thread of silver music adrift in a heavy sea.

* * *

Travis is sitting on the ground in the back

yard, feeding broken bits of cracker to a gray squirrel. The squirrel takes the crumb from Travis's hand, chews rapid-fire, swallows, reaches for another.

"Who's squirrel is that?" Donald asks.

"Nobody's squirrel, Dad. He's wild."

"You shouldn't feed wild things," Donald says. Then, "Shoo!" and the squirrel races to safety up the nearest tree.

"Why not?" Travis asks, not even angry.

"Diseases." Donald sits beside his son, moving stiffly, a man made of sticks, it isn't easy for a man his age to sit lotus on the ground, where did all the springiness go? "Rabies," he says. "Fleas. Germs. Ticks. Invisible things."

Travis smiles. Offers him a cracker.

"Son," says Donald, a hand on the boy's leg, so youthful, so strong, this stride can conquer mountains. "You can't go through life like this, thinking good things all the time. Don't you hear the sirens at night, son?"

"Don't you hear the breeze, Dad? Don't you hear the song of the universe?"

"You should read the news more. War, famine, brutality, perversion. Listen to the police channel on the scanner."

"You should tune into the gaia, Dad. The oneness. Just open yourself to it, and let it in."

"In the course of their lifetime, one in three

21

people will fall victim to a violent crime. One in two marriages will end in divorce. Three out of three people will die."

"Life is a classroom. Some of us learn faster than others."

"But suicide, Travis. Suicide is a negative. A step back. I need you to promise me you will never try it again."

"When I graduated from junior high," Travis says, "first in my class, you were proud of me, weren't you?"

"Of course," Donald says, "But—"

"And when I won the Science Award last year, and sang a solo at District Chorus, and broke the junior varsity scoring record for the most baskets in a single game? You were happy for me, right?"

"I thought to myself, this boy is a wonder. This boy is going to be special."

"I am special, Dad, and so are you. Everybody is somebody special. So please, don't expect me to adhere to your agenda. I have my own itinerary, and I'm anxious to move on. And when I do, I hope you will be just as proud and happy for me as you have always been in the past."

Donald stands quickly, nauseated, voice and knees aquiver. "There are medicines for people who think like that, Travis. There are treatments available. And believe me, I'm your father, and I'm going to protect you whether you like it or not."

*   *   *

There are so many things going on in Donald's life, so many unrelated things to worry about, to fear, that his life feels broken somehow, fragmented, laying about in so many scattered pieces. He is on his hands and knees, naked, trying to crawl away from this mess. Every move cuts deep. Every jagged shard slices flesh, draws blood. A trickle here, a drip there. Here a squirt, there a spurt. He is anemic from all this bleeding. A quart low. Leaking like a sieve. Which way is out? Who hid the door?

*   *   *

Leeanne has been promoted again. When Donald first met her at Jerry's funeral she was a secretary, going to night school and weekend college. She was sobbing when Donald met her, sitting alone in a rear corner of the room, a pretty young thing, petite, stylish, a lace handkerchief dabbing at her eyes. There are at least a dozen such women in similar positions throughout the room, the place is thick with

23

perfume and tears. Donald, at a loss himself, lost in his own fog of grief, comes into the room and sits beside her, sits there for fifteen, twenty minutes before her scent of fuchsia penetrates his clogged sinuses, and he looks away from the casket finally, he turns to her, this woman nearly a child, not quite half his age.

Feeling protective, paternal, moved by her sadness, feeling too alone with his own, he slips an arm around her, she leans into him, they have a drink at the place on the corner, they eulogize Jerry, they go back to her place and make love on the futon.

Now Leeanne sleeps on a kingsized platform bed in a much larger apartment. She has an MBA and is working toward her doctorate. She is the first female vice president in the history of her company. And today she has been promoted to the position of senior vice president, a promotion she tells Donald about while sipping a glass of white wine and watching him wash the breakfast dishes she didn't get around to washing that morning.

"In fact," she says, "I can now afford not only a new car but a housekeeper. Especially if I hire an illegal alien."

"Sounds as if I'm about to lose my job," Donald jokes.

"By the way, did you notice the new door-man downstairs?"

"They seem to get younger everyday, don't they?"

"From the looks of things, he's hung like a horse."

"He's barely out of his teens."

"It sure would be nice to get screwed with some energy for a change."

Leeanne grows meaner with every promotion. She has gone past assertive, beyond ambitious. Donald wonders why he continues to visit her. Why she abides his presence.

"Come and give me a foot massage," she says.

He dries his hands, kneels at her feet, takes one small foot between both hungry palms.

"I've been missing Jerry more than ever lately," he says. "Sometimes I even talk to him as if he's there in the room with me. That's pretty weird, isn't it?"

Leeanne takes a sip of wine, lays her head back, flexes her toes. "In a little over a year I'll have my Ph.D.," she says. "By that time I'll have moved up another rung. I'll be two steps from the top then. Second in line for the presidency."

"Sometimes, I swear, I can actually hear his voice."

"The only ones in my way are Johnson and Mateo. Johnson's an old fart; he's just marking time until retirement. But Mateo, he could be a problem."

"Do you ever think about Jerry these days?"

"Unless, of course. . . . I wonder how a sexual harassment charge would look on Mateo's résumé."

"I really need somebody to talk to these days. My son wants to kill himself. But how can I convince him not to when what I really want is to kill *myself?*"

"Hmmm," Leeanne says, and thinks for a moment. "You know, maybe I should buy my new doorman a little gift. Just to welcome him on board."

* * *

Every night the ritual of locking up. It is barely past nine but to Donald the hour seems late, so late. Jessica is watching TV as he comes home, hangs his jacket in the foyer closet, stands there on the tile, as tired as mud. She is watching a special about sex in the former Soviet Union: one out of three high school girls would do it for money, prostitution ranks eighth in a list of the ten best professions.

Donald stands frozen in the Siberia of his

foyer. He is crumbling like communism. His soul is as empty as a meat market in Minsk.

"Is Travis in?" he asks.

Jessica glances over her shoulder. "Of course." She smiles.

Of course Travis in in. Upstairs in his bedroom, doing homework or surveying the heavens through his telescope. His stereo tuned to an NPR station, to sounds as ethereal as an interstellar chinook, "Music from the Heart of Space," a synthesized orchestration as numbing as sodium pentathol.

Jessica works to keep the accusation from her voice, the fear, and wonders aloud, casually, "Where you been?"

"Driving around," says Donald. "Looking for shots. Ideas. Pictures. You know."

"Find any?"

"Nope."

She half-turns on the sofa now. Lays a hand across the headrest. "Come watch the rest of this with me. It's really interesting."

"As soon as I lock up," he says.

The order of lock-up is very important. Donald does not know why, except that once established, a ritual must be maintained. Or else it is not a ritual at all.

First comes the front door, outside storm

door and then interior wooden door: lock, jiggle; lock, jiggle. Secured. Now through the livingroom to the kitchen and the back door. But on his way Jessica interrupts.

"Could you adjust the color for me?" she asks. "Ted Koppel's been green all night, and I can't get him to look natural."

Donald fiddles with the knobs. "How's this?"

"Better. But now the bushes in Gorky Park are pink."

"It was a red country," says Donald.

"Too much red is just as annoying as too much green. Try turning both knobs at the same time."

It takes him another three minutes to get it right. Now he must return to the front door to go through the motions again. Unlocks the wooden door to jiggle-check the storm door. Closes, locks and jiggle-checks the wooden door. Secured. On to the kitchen once again.

It isn't that he thinks the doors might have come unlocked while he was fiddling with the TV, he isn't that crazy, not yet. But the rhythm has been broken, the natural order. If he had allowed the lock-up ritual to go unrepaired, he would later lie in bed restless, tense, unfinished. He will feel that way anyway, no matter what, but now there will be one less possible cause.

28

"You're obsessive," Jessica says when he returns from locking the back and basement doors.

"I don't disagree," he says, and sits beside her, thighs touching, hers warm, his itchy with guilt. He always fears that he has carried Leeanne's scent home with him, the fragrance of Obsession. Jessica, on the other hand, smells of crushed rose petals.

"You think that makes it okay?" she asks. "That you know your behavior is unnatural?"

"I think it's better than not knowing, don't you?"

"You're neurotic, sweetie."

"I don't mind. Everybody else is neurotic too."

"I'm not."

"A touch paranoid maybe. In a certain endearing way."

"I suppose it's typical of the modern world. To be one or the other."

"A little bit of both is okay too," he says. He slips an arm around her, his life-mate, he will never cheat again. "So what's this show all about?"

"It's about how all the old values of the Soviet Union are disintegrating," she says. "Because of American influence."

"The blind leading the blind," Donald says. "The dead leading the dying."

*   *   *

Jessica and Donald can not agree on the disposition best for their son. Jessica, lying in the middle of their bed, knees raised, Donald undulating langorously atop her like an inchworm caught between two tines of a fork, says "I want him to be happy, but not as happy as he is. I just want to take the edge off his happiness. Could you move a little higher, darling?"

Donald shifts a bit more of his weight forward, a subtle maneuver but one which increases the angle of his dangle by a few degrees, sufficient to elicit from Jessica a mew of pleasure, a purr.

"But you," she continues, "do you *have* to read the newspaper headlines aloud at breakfast? You with your statistics and dire pronouncements. You want him to be miserable."

"Not true. I want him to see the world as it truly is."

"Sometimes I think you're getting bigger down there," she says. "You must be exercising it somewhere I don't know about."

"It's grown fat with angst. Turgid with ennui."

30

"You didn't used to be able to go this long."

"Sometimes I think I can go forever," he says. "It makes me sad."

She, hoping to buoy him, raise his spirits, digs ten fingernails into his buttocks.

"I wonder if maybe it *does* have something to do with sex," he says.

"This *is* sex, Donald. Or maybe you hadn't noticed."

"I mean Travis. His condition. The way he is."

"Don't tell me you're beginning to agree with mother."

"It's not that I think she's wrong about the world, I don't. It's just that her correctness seems excessive. She's too right."

"A little faster now, honey. It's starting."

"It just seems to me that maybe Travis *should* be a bit more preoccupied with sex."

"Oh," she says, knees beginning to twitch now, hands to flutter, "ho boy."

"He should be hiding girlie magazines under his bed. Hanging out at cheerleader practice. Spending too much time in the bathroom."

"Jesus god, oh god oh goodie. Oh give it to me baby, oh give it give it give it ohoohoooh *gawd, Donald!*"

A few moments later they are lying side by

31

side with the sheet pulled up to their necks. Jessica says, staring at the ceiling, "You didn't even come, did you?"

"I think I might have," he says. "I guess I'm not sure."

And Jessica begins to cry. "We have sex more often these days than we have in years," she says. "I have more and better orgasms than ever. And you're not even here!"

"I'm here, Jess. I'm always here."

"You're as far away from me as you can possibly get. You've got a long-distance cock, that's all. You fax me your love."

Donald does not know what to say to this. He hasn't the strength to deny her claim. He adores her, desires only her, wants only her and Travis's happiness. But there is no door he can lock now to keep her fear at bay. He has not yet found the proper ritual that will sanctify his home.

* * *

Donald can not sleep. The rhythym of Jessica's susurrous breathing is broken now and then by the clack of her jaw, teeth grinding. She chews violently on the gristle of her dreams, she gnaws at the flesh and sinew of whatever terrors attend her now.

32

Donald is weary enough in muscle and bone to sleep well into the third millenium, but his soul is as tense as an overstrung guitar wire, vibrating stiffly, one more pluck and it will snap. Besides, he has his own dreams to avoid. He slides in darkness off the side of the bed, pausing for a moment on his haunches, not wanting to disturb his wife, to deprive her of whatever small amnesia her sleep obtains. He feels for his trousers on the floor, can't find them, gives up, tiptoes in his underwear into the hallway.

Outside Travis's bedroom he pauses, listens, then peeks inside, gliding the door open by another four inches. There is his child on the moonbathed bed, Travis stretched out as long as the mattress yet still just a baby, as innocent as a newborn.

Oh son, Donald thinks, and stops the tears only because he knows they will do him no good. Where did I fail you, my boy? Somebody please tell me what I didn't do right.

He remembers Travis's birth, the prolonged labor, interminable fear. The baby, this unknown quality, invisible thing, is stuck sideways in the birth canal, lodged indelibly, it won't come forward and it can't go back. The umbilical cord is a noose around its neck. With every contraction, as Jessica is jolted rigid, shocked out of her pain stupor momentarily, the noose cinches tighter. A heart monitor, its electrodes plugged somehow to the baby's buried skull, beeps. Every now and then a beep is skipped, and when this happens, Donald's heart skips too. Gasps. Holds its breath until the monitor beeps again.

The number of beeps per minute, Travis's heartrate, is diminishing. One hundred sixteen. One hundred twelve. The noose pulls tighter, strangling, choking. Is the unknown quality in pain? Does it know fear? One hundred four. Ninety-nine. The doctor's eyes, all that is visible of his face beneath blue cap and above blue mask, the eyes look worried, bright with ominous concern. He has been working for over an hour now. He is losing confidence, losing resolve, it shows in his eyes. *Get her upstairs!* Donald wants to scream. *What are you waiting for, do a ceasarian!* Jessica is beyond pain now, the pain its own narcotic, her hand in his is limp.

The doctor says "Get me the suction" and one of the nurses scurries to produce it. It is a strange-looking contraption, the rubber cup of a plumber's helper attached to the truncated handle of an old-fashioned handpump. What mad scientist thought up this torture device?

The doctor disconnects the electrodes from the baby's skull. The heart monitor falls silent, a din as loud as death. The doctor works the suction cup inside Jessica. She groans vaguely. He attaches the cup to the slippery small head. Then pumps furiously on the handle, increasing suction pressure until Donald feels his own heart ballooning, about to burst. Then slowly, firmly, the doctor begins to pull, easing the contraption toward his chest.

Progress stops suddenly. He cuts a look toward Donald, eyes glassy with . . . what? Then another tug, and *pop!* the slimy red baseball of a head appears. And an instant later *whoosh!* a slippery purple body, a skinned squirrel.

The doctor unclamps, snips, syringes, wipes, and lays the ugly viscuous thing on Jessica's chest. "Here's your fella," the doctor says. "Here's your little guy."

Donald is blubbering, he kisses the slimy face, the bloody forehead, he kisses Jessica and smears the blood across her sweatslick cheek. "It's a boy," he sobs, trying to convince himself, to believe.

The baby's skull is shaped like a cone, a dunce's cap.

"From the suction," the doctor explains. "It will go back to normal in a day or two."

Donald leans away to catch his breath. He is hyperventilating. The baby, Travis, has not uttered a single cry. "Travis honey," Donald gasps, and holds the slippery hand, "it's me, baby, it's your daddy."

Travis turns his head toward Donald, he opens his eyes, he smiles.

"Well will you look at that!" the doctor says.

* * *

There is a message on Donald's answering machine. Donald is on his way to the dark-room, barechested, barefoot, to talk with Jerry's filmy image on the wall, to commune, when in passing he glances at the answering machine, sees the signal light. He rewinds the tape, plays it back, and listens stunned to Wright's voice speaking as if from the grave, from some damp and foggy Aberglaube.

"Hey buddy, how you doin' these days. . . . Listen . . . I'm sorry about never answering your calls . . . never picking up. I appreciate your concern, I really do. . . .

"Hell, I . . . I know you just want to help, Don. Not that anybody can help, not unless you're Christ himself, or you've got a miracle cure up your sleeve. But I know you *want* to, and that's a good thing to know. That in itself helps, it really does. Having a friend like you. It helps a lot.

"So anyway. I'm feeling better these days, relatively speaking. For awhile there I was pretty badly off. I couldn't eat, couldn't urinate, couldn't defecate, I was sleeping maybe ten minutes at a shot. Then I had a little stopgap work done, just to open things up temporarily. I felt so good for a week or so, I almost called to invite you out to a twi-night double-header. In the end, though, I went by myself. Boy, was that a mistake! I came home after the fourth inning. Those hard seats, I just couldn't take it. And all those people. The noise. I never felt more alone. . . .

"It's a weird feeling, knowing you're dying. Feeling it happening all the time. It's like. . . .

"Remember being a kid, a teenager, and going to the sock hop? Getting up against a girl for the very first time?

"Remember falling in love with some sweet warm thing whose name you didn't know? And not working up the nerve to ask her to dance until the very last song? And then finally getting her in your arms? and listening to the music? feeling it in your blood? and knowing it was going to end any second now, it was all going to end, all that delicious warm

37

fear of feeling her heart thumping against your own. . .?

"That's sort of what this thing is like, bud. This is the last dance. And I've finally got her in my arms, the Big Blonde, the one I've been watching for a long time now. The music is playing and she's pressed up against me and I'm as nervous as a teenager, you know? She's all hot and sweaty from dancing all night, and there's this scent of sweat and cheap perfume she's giving off, the perfume is called Musk, remember that stuff?

"I'm so fucking dizzy with the scent and the heat of her, I don't know if this is love or what. All I know is that the music is going to end sooner or later, it has to. So in the meantime. . . .

"Don't try cutting in on us, Don. I love you, man, I really do, but this is something else entirely. . . .

"I'm holding onto this one until the lights go out.

"I'm going home with her.

"Christ, she scares me."

*   *   *

"What's it like where you are?" Donald asks. And Jerry says, "Gray."

"Gray?"

"More of an off-white, I guess. Eggshell."

"Geez," Donald says.

"How about if I ask a question now?"

"Be my guest."

"What's your favorite instrument?"

"What does that have to do with anything?"

"I'm taking a survey, okay?"

"The saxophone."

"Why the saxophone?"

"Why?" says Donald. "I don't know. Because it has a ropy kind of quality, I guess. It sounds like something I could swing on. Something I could climb on, like a kid. Something I could shinny up, out of sight, do the Indian rope trick on."

"What's bugging you, my friend? Talk."

"Everything."

"Be specific."

"I don't care what day it is."

"And that worries you?"

"You don't think it should?"

"Today is Friday."

"You see? You see how little that news affects me? I simply do not care, one way or the other, that today is Friday."

"And why should you? You don't have an employer to work overtime for, you don't

39

watch Saturday morning cartoons, you don't attend religious services. Every day is just a day. Nameless, without distinction. There are no divisions of weeks for you. No months."

"Right. So how can there be so many years? So many years behind me?"

"It does strain one's credulity, doesn't it?"

"Can I tell you something else, Jer?"

"That's why I'm here, pal."

"I hear things."

"So you're not deaf, count your blessings."

"Often I hear a kind of dull muffled roaring in the sky."

"Thunder, that's what it is."

"On a perfectly sunny day. Not a cloud, not a hint of gray."

"A jet then. The Concorde, for example, way up in the upper stratosphere."

"It's not a jet, not even the Concorde. The intonation isn't right. Or the pitch, the modulation, whatever you call it. I know a jet when I hear one."

"The jet stream then. Wafting down from Ottawa. Racing up from Waco."

"There are other things too. When I'm in the shower, I hear the phone ringing. The doorbell. People screaming for help."

"Water in your ears."

"Often I have the feeling of being watched."

"Typical of the times."

"A savage insatiable lust. I want to fuck everybody, but nobody appeals to me."

"Nonspecific urethritis. A mild inflammation. Too much caffeine in your piss."

"Does prayer really work?"

"Cranberry juice works better."

"Is there a God?"

"I've heard certain rumors."

"Are you in Heaven or Hell?"

"It's *your* darkroom, pal. You decide."

*   *   *

Donald is sitting at his breakfast table, a mug of black coffee in his hands as he stares out the window at his parcel of lawn, his driveway, his neighbor's lawn and driveway, neighbor after neighbor, lawn and driveway after lawn and driveway.

Jessica and Deirdre are seated across from him, talking, mother's and daughter's voices so similar as to sometimes blur into one. He doesn't want to look at either of them just now, the morning is too new, unformed, he hasn't the stomach yet for interaction, for facing the mirrors in their eyes.

Donald gazes out the window and wishes

there were some mountains in his life, a range of purple majesty upon which to fix his gaze, on which to hang his thoughts. He wants not figurative mountains, not the lofty slopes of dreams nor the perfect peaks of poetry, he wants dirt and rock piled high, stratum upon stratum, epoch upon epoch. The Rockies. Sierra Madres. The Grand Tetons. Mount St. Helens.

"I read once," he says aloud, not knowing there are words in his mouth until he hears them roll out, "that people who can gaze out their windows and see a mountain or two live longer and happier lives."

From across the narrow table comes silence. Jessica stares at him and wonders something, he can only guess what.

"Longer and happier than what?" Deirdre asks. "Than whom?"

"Than people who can see only plain. Desert. Pasture-land. Lawn."

"I can understand that," says Jessica, ever the ally, peacemaker to the world. "The beauty of nature. The panoramic view."

"Some people are city people," Deirdre says.

"Concrete walls," Donald muses. "Curtains of carbon monoxide. Windows full of bald-headed mannequins who have forgotten how to smile."

42

"Reminds me of somebody I know," says Deirdre. Then, "Anyway, place is unimportant. It's what's inside that matters. Faith. A belief in something bigger."

"Mountains are bigger," says Donald. "A lot bigger." He is looking at his neighbor's lawnball now.

"Faith can move mountains," says Deirdre.

"I believe what I can see."

There is an argument brewing, so Jessica hurries to lower the heat. "In a sense," she says, "you are both talking about the same thing. To gaze upon a mountain is to feel a sense of awe. To experience the magnificence of nature. In that regard, to merely gaze upon a mountain is a form of worship. An exercise in faith."

"If you *need* the physical reassurance," Deirdre says. "If you aren't capable of finding it within yourself."

"I'd like to photograph some mountains," Donald says.

Deirdre tells him, "It's been done."

"Everything's been done," he counters, blood pressure rising now, veins beginning to bulge.

"I'll tell you something that hasn't been done," Deirdre says, and gets up to pour herself another cup of coffee. "That grandson of mine hasn't been put on the right track yet."

Donald stiffens, about to respond, to reach

43

for the cutlery. But he is disarmed suddenly by Jessica's hand squeezing his, her smile, the light of forgiveness ever glinting in her eyes.

He squeezes her hand in return, then stands, heads for the back door, tossing over his shoulder a petulant, "If faith really can move mountains, Deirdre, how come I never see you levitating back home?" And he ducks quickly outside, the only way to win.

*   *   *

Donald and Wright once made a book together. Photographs by Donald, text by Wright. A coffeetable book. *A Nature Walk,* they called it. Brilliant color photographs of a waterfall limned with crystal ice. Spring cowlilies pushing through the dirt. A murderous-eyed Cooper's hawk perched on the spear of a dead swamp tree.

Each photograph is accompanied by a short poem. Each poem is rigidly structured, metered, rhymed. Amateurish and sentimental. Unpublishable.

An editor telephones Donald a few days after one of the book's many rejections. "Let me hook you up with another writer," he says. "A professional. Your photographs are wonderful. I would love to work with you on this."

For seven years now a copy of the unpublished book has languished in a box in Donald's basement, collecting the scent of mold. Wright has a copy too, which he keeps sending out. He shows Donald the rejection slips. Thirty-nine so far. Donald never asks to see them, never mentions the project unless Wright brings it up, which he hasn't done for several months.

These days, lately, one of the unproductive things Donald does alone in his basement office is to hold that moldering book in his lap, turn the thick pages and look at the photographs and wonder who the man with the camera was. That middle-aging boy able to fill a frame with the blue beauty of a flower the size of his thumbnail. Able to make a frozen waterfall resonate off the page with the music of a glass celesta, the tinkle of icicles falling. Able to find the cosmos in a dew-sequined cobweb, the sanity in a star.

That boy, whomever he was, Donald has lost him, that life-loving boy. Did he die with the first rejection, or the twentieth? What experience or fear made him doubt his eye for the beautiful, made him suspicious of the stirrings of his heart? When did he lose his passion, his drive? When did his talent go belly-up?

Donald, so lonely, Donald wishes he knew.

* * *

Kittenfaced girls and ratfaced boys. Ortho-donture by the acre. Baggy loud clothes and shoes untied, thirty dollar haircuts, this is what Donald sees in the city, in the park, as he sits on a bench with his Lieca in his hands. Children are so tall these days, so loud. How can sperm and ova go so awry? Was he ever this arrogant, this sure of himself?

Don't dwell on it, Donald. Look elsewhere.

There, for example. The water-fountain shaped like a lion's head. That tiny tyke want-ing a drink. Cute little towheaded boy climbing into the lion's mouth, dragging himself up. Ah, success! He beams, grins proudly, now kneels on the fiberglass mandible and leans forward for a drink.

Donald raises the camera to his eye. A lovely picture. His finger on the button. But wait. Sure the boy is happy now, he's innocent, he doesn't know a thing. But someday he will look up from his comic book to see Daddy sock Mommy in the eye. He'll see Uncle Freddie gunned down in a drive-by shooting. Somebody will poison his dog. A cloud of toxic waste will hang over his neighborhood, dust his tricycle, shimmer in

46

his sandbox. His parents will send him to Clear-water, Florida to live in a trailer park with Granny, who supplements her social security check by selling tiny bags of white powder, but somewhere over King's Island, while the boy is nibbling on a bag of peanuts and watching the sea of clouds below, a swarthy man sitting three rows ahead will mutter a prayer to Allah, and the Boeing 737 will explode.

Donald lowers the camera. He holds it bloodless on his knee. He takes no picture, ex-poses no film to the glare of this day, to its sunny scarification, its sere illusion of laughter and hope.

*   *   *

"I've been having such weird dreams lately."

"It is the nature of dreams to be weird, is it not?"

"In this one, I'm walking through the city at night, and I get lost, and I end up in a blind alleyway."

"The symbolism's fairly sophomoric here, if you don't mind my saying so."

"Out of nowhere comes a big ugly mugger. He rips the camera from my hands, then stands there looking at it, like a gorilla or something who can't understand what a camera is for. So I pull out my wallet and I say Here, take it all, take everything I've got, just please don't take my camera."

"And he eats the camera, right?"

"He takes my wallet, but then he hurls the camera against a wall. When it breaks, pieces fly off into space like pieces from an exploding kaleidoscope. The mugger punches me a good one in the belly, and then he turns and walks away laughing, until he disappears in the darkness."

"Did you recognize the mugger as anybody you know? Your father, maybe? Your high school sweetheart?"

"Wait, I'm coming to that. So anyway, when I get my breath back I stumble out to the street. It's daylight now, a bright winter afternoon, the sun is as bright as burnished metal. There's a cop at the intersection directing traffic, so I hustle over to him, dodging cars, nearly getting run over a couple of times. And I tell him I've been mugged. He takes out a pad and pencil and asks for a description of my assailant. And I say Well, he was of medium height, brown hair, green eyes, he was wearing a red and yellow flannel shirt, blue jeans and a pair of dirty sneakers. The cop stops writing and stands there looking at me strangely. And that's when I realize—"

"You've given him a description of yourself."

"He reaches for his billy club, so I start running again, upstreet through the traffic, weaving in and out between cars. Meanwhile the cop is hot on my tail and now *he's shooting at me!* Bullets are flying everywhere. Ricochetting off the pavement, pinging off car doors, thunking into pedestrians. People are dropping like flies. The gutters become rivers of blood. Me, I'm running like crazy for the river, don't ask me why, but that's where I feel I need to go. My lungs are on fire, my legs are like mud, and the cop keeps getting closer and closer. And he never runs out of ammunition!"

"I bet I know who the cop looks like."

"What's it all mean, I wonder."

"Did the cop eventually catch you?"

"I make it to the river, but now it isn't winter anymore, it's summer. And the river is the Caribbean Ocean. And I'm trapped there on the beach, caught between the water and the policeman, whose bullets are nicking me with regularity now. And just when I think I'm dead for sure, all of a sudden you come swooping in above the beach in your parasail, and you scoop me up off the sand like a hawk snatching a rabbit."

"Interesting simile."

"And you carried me up into the sky. Higher

49

and higher we went. So high I eventually couldn't even hear the cop shooting at me anymore. The clouds kept getting thicker and thicker, and they smelled like antiseptic, like a hospital room. I looked up at you and yelled, Where are you taking me, Jer? And when I said that, we all of a sudden stopped moving. We just hovered there for a moment. When you looked down at me, your face was sad, and a little bit angry. And you said, You had to ask, didn't you? And then you dropped me. I guess I woke myself up screaming. Jessica didn't wake up, though, so I guess I only dreamed I was screaming."

"Too bad you woke up. It might have been interesting to see where you landed."

"Why did you drop me, Jerry?"

"It seemed the natural thing to do."

* * *

"I don't feel like sex tonight," Donald says.

And Leeanne, who in her living room has already begun to disrobe, pantyhose peeled to her knees, says, "What do you mean you don't feel like sex?"

"I don't feel like sex."

"Well I feel like sex."

"So okay, no problem. We'll have sex."

"That's why you're here, isn't it? Sex is why you're here."

"It's not only sex."

"We've never not had sex."

"Sex isn't everything."

"It's six o'clock Tuesday night. Every Tuesday night at six o'clock, we have sex."

"Sex on a timetable."

"I don't care if it's on a coffeetable, I'm ready for sex. I brushed my teeth for sex, I've psychologically programmed myself for sex, I've cleared my schedule for sex. And I fully expect that, one hour from now, I will be heating up my microwave dinner for one while still all aflush in the relaxing afterglow of a satisfying session of sex."

Donald stands and smiles. "Let there be sex."

* * *

"Hey bud," the phone message says, "how's it hangin'?" Wright's voice as soft and damp as moss coming from the plastic box is a peculiar kind of frightening; there is terror in that voice, an understated terror that pricks the hair on Donald's arms, a chill that makes his nipples sore.

"Boy, am I glad you don't have one of those

51

machines that cuts a guy off after thirty seconds. I never know what I'm going to say until I say it."

But there is another quality to the voice as well, a resignation, wide-eyed and awestruck, a kamikaze kind of eagerness for the terror. Donald hugs himself, plucks his glasses off. The world of his basement becomes a frosty blur.

"I bet after that last message of mine you think I've lost it, don't you?"

There is a brief liquid sound, muffled slurp, followed by a clink. Is Wright drinking a beer? Scotch on the rocks? Donald wants to know.

"But I'll tell you something, Don. This is strange but . . . I don't know, maybe it's not so strange after all. Maybe it's only natural. . . .

"Let's say I look out my window in the morning. You know the Somerfields across the street? That bed of peonies and mums around their front porch? Well I can smell those flowers, bud. I mean from behind my bedroom window, I can really smell them! It's weird. . . .

"I can taste things I haven't tasted since I was a kid. Coffee soup, for example. Do you know what that is? My old man used to make it for breakfast when I was a boy. All I have to do now is to think about it, and *I can fucking taste it.* And all the while I can smell our old coal furnace on a winter morning, just like I'm sitting there by the register the way I used to. . . .

"And then yesterday? I was lying on my bed in the afternoon? Just thinking about nothing in particular, I guess. Trying to make my mind a blank. And you know what I heard, Don? Not imagined, but *heard?* I heard a violin playing. Honest to God I did. It was as if Itzak Perlman himself were sitting there on the edge of my bed, it was that real. And it wasn't coming from outside, or from a radio, or anything like that. It was coming *out of the air.*

"It must have lasted for, I don't know, fifteen or twenty seconds before it stopped. It stopped the very moment I consciously realized that I was listening to something . . . what? Unearthly?

"But it was so beautiful, Don. It was like . . . too beautiful, you know?

"I actually cried."

There is a long pause now. The sounds of Wright soothing his throat, a long swallow. He shifts the telephone to his other ear, Donald hears it in the tone change of dead air.

"Anyway, bud. About that last message of mine. About the Big Blonde, remember?"

Wright pauses. He chuckles softly, hoarsely.

"Remember how awkward I always was around women? Well, no more, my friend. No more."

In the next long silence Donald feels a chill ripple through him. His spine tingles. He feels not alone in the room; watched. He puts on his glasses and looks all around but there is nobody with him, no form nor shadow nor gauzy mist undulating in the air.

"She's kind of gross, Don, to be perfectly honest about it. She's no cover girl, that's for sure. But I don't know, she's got something appealing about her, some kind of animal sexiness, I don't know what it is.

"She's a big woman. Bigboned. A couple of inches taller than me.

"She's got a wide mouth and red juicy lips, very red. Huge green eyes that sometimes bulge a little, like a lizard's maybe.

"Pendulous, soft breasts. Big tits, bud, seriously big.

"She wears too much powder on her face, it's too white, but even so I can see the pores on her cheeks. Pores as big as blackheads. And the hotter she gets, the bigger the pores open up. Like when we're dancing, you know? And she's rubbing up against me, and her hands are flying all over my back, she's getting sweaty and hot and those big pores of hers are as big as . . . it's almost like she's breathing through them. Jesus, it makes me warm."

The longest pause of the night now, the chillest silence. Donald's naked chest is a contour map of goosebumps and rigid hair follicles. Wright's voice when it returns is different again, flatter, solemner, the voice of a dying man.

"Listen, bud. You haven't told Jessie any of this stuff, have you? I don't want you to. And I mean *any* of it, I don't want her to know a thing. Remember, you promised.

"I figure she doesn't know yet or she'd have been over here by now breaking in the windows and force-feeding me chicken soup, that's the kind of girl she is. You're a lucky man, Donny, to have a woman like her. And a great kid like Travis. You've always been lucky. You were born to win. . . .

"Anyway, friend, don't tell Jess about any of this, okay? I know how much it would hurt her. It shouldn't but I know it would. I don't want it to hurt you either, okay? I mean it, don't feel bad about this. All I really want from you is . . . I don't know.

"I just want somebody to understand."

* * *

"It's all muddied up in sex, isn't it?" Donald asks.

"What is?"

"Everything. Love, death, ambition, power. . . ."

"We're sexy little creatures, no denying the obvious. Was, in my case."

"How many women in all, Jer?"

"Including after St. Croix?"

"There's sex after death?"

"I've heard it referred to as such, but there are more differences now than similarities. Anyway, as for the number of women I knew physically, I don't remember. Statistics, they're the first things to go."

"A hundred and something, that's what you told me once."

"Over fifty times more than Wright had, geez. And he's the one with the ballooning prostate."

"Looking back, Jer, now that you've achieved a different perspective, now that you're some distance from it, or so I assume— What I mean is, it seemed to me that sex was, in a way, your primary motive for living. It was all you ever talked about, all you cared about, all you *did*, for chrissakes. Looking back, what do you think of all that now?"

"I think you've asked me a damn long-winded question."

"But as for sex. . .?"

"It's a fun way to spend an hour. But it's not important. It is no great accomplishment to get laid."

"Then your life. . . ."

"I wasted my life. Getting one's rocks off is dismally small justification for all the money and time and energy I invested in pursuit of an activity even troglodytes were adept at."

"Then you don't think Travis should be more interested in sex?"

"What makes you think you know what Travis is or isn't interested in?"

"You're right. I don't."

"And while we're on the subject of sex, let me ask you this. What is your attraction to that woman?"

"To Jess?"

"Don't be coy."

"Leeanne. Hmmm. Well. . . ."

"You can't hold onto me through her, my friend. She's a different woman than the one I knew."

"I would certainly hope so."

"You think you deserve the abuse she heaps on you, right?"

"Just look at me, Jer. I'm a failure. I'm a schmo."

"What exactly is it you want from life, Donald?"

"What do I want?"

"All of us want something. Even Gandhi did. Even Christ. Me, I wanted to make a ton of money and get laid more often than Johnny Wad. But I don't think I ever understood what *you* want."

"I guess what I want is to know what I want."

"Dig deep into your psyche, boy. Probe until it hurts."

"I want Travis to be happy in ways that do not involve suicide. I want Jessie to know how much I love her. I want Deirdre to quit making such a pest of herself. I want Leeanne to realize that being an independent woman doesn't mean she has to squash every testicle she can get her hands on. I want Wright to wake up tomorrow with a healthy prostate. And I want you, Jer, I want you to be alive and well and kicking my ass in racquetball, just the way you used to."

"But what about for you? What do you want for Donald?"

"All those things are for me."

"I mean just for you. For you and nobody else. Be honest, kid. What is it you want?"

"I don't want to be erased like a misspelled word."

* * *

There had once burned in him a passion as pure as flame.

There once shone a light so brilliant as to blind him to all the obstacles to his ideal. But the flame is lower now, it barely keeps him warm. The light is dimmer, no longer a beacon, but a tiny distant star.

He has made a compromise with mediocrity. He has turned away from that original fire of ambition, that passion to be strong and brave and alone, a voice above the crowd. He was turned away finally by an inferior kind of hunger. Seduced away by the lure of easy comfort. Suckered away by self-doubt and loneliness and fatigue, his voice grown hoarse from too much shouting toward which too few listeners ever turned to hear.

He has a talent but he does not do his most to nurture it. He gives himself too many rests. He looks too closely at what the world wants, what it rewards, and he culls back his own expectations so as to reap some of those rewards. And so the rage in him becomes two-sided; the handle of the knife he holds becomes itself a blade.

He assumes responsibility for others before fulfilling responsibilities to himself. He becomes an old man half a lifetime early. Old because he has given in to what he despises. Old because he has ceased to believe the impossible. Old because he has lost all faith in the sparkling beauty of his dreams.

*   *   *

Donald is dreaming about Travis as a little boy, Travis is four, he and Donald and Jessica are camping fifty yards back from a fast and muddy river. Their tent is as big as a cabin and bright yellow and Jessica is seated near the campfire, popping popcorn. It is dusk, nearly dark, a gray August night. The only colors are those illuminated by the fire, everything else in varied shades of gray or black. Travis moves between the tent and the noisy river, gathering wildflowers. Donald in his dream has trouble locating himself. Is he there at all? Yes, there he is, over there, he is standing upriver. Doing what? Doing nothing. Staring at the muddy rush of water, the endless churn of brown.

Suddenly Jessica screams. Donald pivots.

She is rigid, a fire-lit spectre of absolute fear, finger pointing toward the river. With one sweeping glance uninterrupted by the figure of a boy Donald knows what has happened and he dives in, he flings himself far out into the thick swirling chill. Stroking hard, kicking hard, Donald struggles to keep his head high as the hard current whisks him past the campsite, his eyes fighting mud and darkness. *Travis!* he cries gurgling, *Travis honey where are you? Daddy's coming!* But there is no reply, no shadow of a small bobbing head to break the roiled surface.

And now somehow Donald is on shore, wet clothes heavy and cold as he races madly through a thicket, jagged branches snapping like whips against his face, twigs stabbing his head, *Get me a flashlight! I can't see anything!*, and he is nearly crazy with the terror of loss, directionless, he doesn't know where to look, to run.

Now he is on a high stone bridge peering down and he thinks *this is like a dream* and yes! there goes Travis clinging to a log shooting by beneath the bridge. *Daddy's coming honey hang on!* and feetfirst into the river Donald goes, *I've got him now, I'll save him now.*

But instead of bobbing abruptly to the surface Donald's body continues speeding down, a torpedo cutting through the muck, he scoops wildly and kicks but he cannot reverse his descent, he is a mile below the surface and still diving, eyeglasses torn off, irretrievable, he had no idea the river is so deep.

He strikes something hard now, he stops, he has bottomed out finally and is standing in the mud. He needs air, his lungs are about to burst, he will never make it to the top. That hard slick object he struck, it is a pale blur beside him but he examines it quickly with his hands and recognizes it finally as a refrigerator, a 19 cu.ft. Frigidaire frost-free with automatic ice-maker wedged obliquely in the sediment. Donald wrestles frantically with the door, it is stuck firm but then pops open, the sucking sound of decompression, he dives inside and the door whooshes shut and he sticks his muddy head out the tentflap just as the popcorn begins to pop and Jessica seated alone dressed all in black beside the blurry fire looks at him impassively and says *There's none for you, don't even ask.*

* * *

"You can't keep doing this, you know."
"I'm too tense to go back to sleep."
"That's no excuse for talking to a dead man."

"But I enjoy this, it relaxes me. . . . Your voice gets clearer day by day."

"You'd better stop while you can."

"I really miss you, Jerry."

"Talk to somebody alive for a change. Pick one!"

"I'm annoying you."

"You think this is all I have to do? You think *I* don't have problems of my own?"

"My dreams are destroying my life."

"Contraria contrariis curantur, my friend."

"Come again?"

"Fix your life and you'll fix your dreams."

"It's not my life that troubles me, it's Travis's."

"Haven't been reading your Jung lately, have you?"

"You think Travis in the dream was me."

"The boy in you, sí."

"But . . . I can't concentrate enough to figure this out."

"How old are you, Donald?"

"I'm forty-four."

"Try again."

"According to my birth certificate I am."

"Paper lies. How old do you feel?"

"Twelve? Ten? Maybe younger."

"You are a confused, uneducated boy."

"I know the alphabet but I don't know how to spell."

"You can't read, can't fathom the concept of time, can't speak plainly enough to make yourself understood."

"I'm three, I guess. I'm one."

"You don't know where you came from, have no idea where you're going. The notions of *beginning* and *end* make you dizzy."

"I'm an embryo. A squiggly newt."

"You try to consider the *self*, but the mind cannot look at itself. It casts no reflection."

"I'm in two places at once. I'm an egg and a sperm."

"Neither can conceive of the other and yet both feel incomplete."

"I'm a cell, I'm a molecule. I'm an atom. I'm a quark."

"How old are you, Donald?"

"I'm too old to remember."

"How old are you, Donald?"

"I am yet to be born."

*　*　*

Leeanne reposes like a Siamese cat on a downstuffed chaise in her livingroom. Her red and yellow flowered silk kimono hangs open to reveal one leg bare to the thigh, the other

naked to the knee. She holds in her limp hanging hand a blackstemmed flute of champagne,
on her face the sleepy satisfied look of one su-
periorly fucked, supremely screwed, the thor-
oughbred lathered from its Kentucky Derby
win, the greyhound star of Sarasota, Queen of
the Honeybees, Empress of the World.

Donald has not yet laid a hand on her. Not
so much as a buss on the cheek. He sits across
the room from her, just inside the door,
perches tenuously on the edge of a hardbacked
chair as he stares woodenly at Leeanne's naked
foot, toes twitching rhythmically, nails as
bright as blood.

"You should see how big my new orifice is,"
she says.

Did he hear that correctly? Was it *orifice* or
office?

"Mateo is fucked now and he knows it," she
says. "I've got them all by the balls."

Donald looks up hoping to identify this room,
to place this woman somewhere in his memory,
find a reason for his presence here. Leeanne has
exposed a breast to him, is circling the nipple
with a forefinger dipped in champagne.

"Come get a taste," she says.

It is a lovely breast, in a detached kind of
way. Donald stands, distantly interested, re-

motely aroused. She opens her robe, holds the flute inclined above her pubic hair, dribbles a dribble of champagne onto the black thatched roof of her corporate hideaway, a shimmer of fruity rain.

Donald unbuckles his trousers although aware that he has no erection. He wants to fuck until he dies but his pecker is dozing soundly. He is a plumber without a plunger, a mechanic sans screwdriver, a toolist devoid of tool.

Donald kneels at the foot of the chaise lounge. Leeanne lifts off his glasses, lays them aside. She raises her ass to him, with one hand pulls his face into her champagne-shampooed hair.

Donald feels so heavy with sadness, the taste of her brings tears to his eyes. He hugs her buttocks and tries to forget whom they are attached to. He hugs her warmth and tries to forget the icy heart.

"So do something," she says hoarsely, the slippery lips lapping at his face. "Use your tongue."

Donald is thinking of Jessica now, her soft beauty in bed. The heartbreaking frown she wears sleeping while he, nearly every night these days, tiptoes away, downstairs to his

room full of negatives, his undeveloped
thoughts. How many times has he stolen past
the bed, wanting to wake her tenderly by doing just this, by slipping his tongue inside her,
dying between her thighs?

". . . a huge mahogany desk," Leeanne is
murmuring. "Plus mahogany filing cabinets.
A wet bar. A view Mateo would kill for." She
purrs throatily, chuckles throatily, a dangerous laugh.

Donald realizes suddenly that his plumber's
helper has sprung awake. That the only way he
can make love to his mistress is by fantasizing
about his wife.

He pulls away, stands up, zips up, blinking,
dazed, and plucks a hair off his tongue.

"Get with it, mister," Leeanne growls
through her teeth. "Your tongue or your dick,
let's see some action."

She is fuzzy around the edges, her face a
blur. Donald leans closer, squinting. "Where
did you put my glasses?"

She holds up the champagne flute. His eyeglasses are submerged inside, bubbly. He
reaches for it but she pulls away. "Not until
you've done your duty."

He lunges for the flute, misses, splats on his
face, white shag up his nose.

"What's your problem?" Leeanne wants to know.

Donald addresses the floor. "I don't like you," he says, "and I want to go home."

Leeanne takes a moment to consider this, assimilate, formulate, extrapolate. Calmly, with executive aplomb, she stands. Marches into the kitchen. Pours the champagne from her glass into the sink. Lays Donald's eyeglasses inside a marble mortar, grips the phallic-shaped pestle, grinds his lenses to dust.

Carrying the mortar, she returns to him. Stands with one foot on each side of his head. Pours the dust of his eyeglasses like snow on his chest.

"Let's see you go home now, asshole."

Donald studies the glitter of broken light that has fluttered atop his hands. "Those glasses were guaranteed unbreakable," he says.

Leeanne returns to the chaise now. She yanks open her robe, flops down, knees raised, legs slightly spread. Donald stands, shimmering splinters raining to the floor. "From now on," Leeanne announces, "I tell you when you can come, and I tell you when you can go. Understood?"

Donald nods once. Then he turns. Through the blur of his myopia he moves, walking and swimming, an underwater flamingo, toward what he presumes and hopes is the door.

"And where the hell do you think you're going?"

It is the door! The knob, the lovely knob, he pulls it toward his groin.

"You get your pathetic ass back here, mister. I'm not through with you yet!"

Donald swims out into the hallway, the night. He locates his car finally by feeling and squinting his way up the street. Drives by instinct, astigmatic homing pigeon, swerving to avoid sudden blurs. He side-swipes only two street signs along the way, destroys only one headlight.

Wobbling like a tenth-round knockout he enters his home, breathes the sweet stuffy air, and shuffles toward the glow of the television set.

"Where are your glasses?" fuzzy Jessica asks.

"I wrecked the car," says Donald.

"My god!"

"Just a minor thing, a little dent. I swerved to . . . miss hitting a dog. And I bumped into a street sign."

She is coming toward him now, concerned. "Did you hit your head or something? What happened to your glasses?"

"Well," he begins, but now she is picking something off his shirt.

"What's this stuff all over you? Why, it's . . . it's glass, isn't it? It looks like powdered glass."

"When I plowed into the street sign," Donald says, "the impact drove my head against the window. Not my head actually, just the corner of my glasses. And when that happened, the glasses flew off, see, and they hit the dashboard, and well, it was the strangest thing, Jess, the lenses just exploded."

"My god," she says again. Her fingers are in his hair now, feeling for a lump.

"I've got an extra pair downstairs."

"Wait," she says. She leans close and sniffs his cheek. "Have you been drinking?"

"I had a quick one afterward. Just to steady my nerves."

She continues to sniff. "You smell like perfume too."

"The accident," he says, "gave me a nosebleed. Some woman came by on the street and lent me her handkerchief."

"Let me see," she says, and stands directly under his nose.

"There's no more blood, I cleaned my nose in the bar where I had a drink. Now let me go please. I need my other glasses."

In the basement, in a drawer in his battered

desk, he finds them. Oh, the world is too sharp-edged and bright! It lacerates the soul.

Jessica calls down from the top of the stairs. "Need any help?"

"Found them," he says.

"Are you coming back up?"

"In a minute or two."

"Maybe we should have a doctor look you over. Okay?"

"I'm fine, dear," he says. "It was just a bloody nose, no big deal."

"Why don't you come up to bed now?"

"You go ahead, I'm just going to check my messages first. Is Travis home?"

"Of course," she says.

"I'll be up in a few minutes, sweetie."

She says nothing more, pauses, waits, then wanders softly away. He hears the television click off, hears Jessica's footsteps padding up to the second floor.

Donald sits on the worn sofa. Sags in the middle. He takes off his glasses, leans back, closes his eyes, picks a fleck of glass off his scalp. He feels, somehow, that he has escaped with his life. A strange kind of victor. Survivor of a very stupid war.

* * *

"Just a short message tonight, bud.

71

"I'm feeling really tired tonight. . . .

"I bet you wonder why I never seem to call when you're in, don't you? Well, it's funny. But I can tell, I mean I just seem to know somehow. I sit here with my hand on the phone, and I think about calling you, and I can *sense* whether you're there or not. If you are, I wait awhile and try again later. It's weird, isn't it?

"I'm discovering all kinds of strange abilities I never knew I had. . . .

"Anyway, I don't want you to get the idea I'm still angry because you followed me that day. Or that I don't want to talk to you. Jesus, I want to talk to you so badly, Don. I just . . . can't. You know?

"In a way, though, that's what these messages are all about. I mean I *am* talking to you, right? And lots of times . . . lots of times it's as if I can even hear you talking back to me. It's like a real conversation almost.

"I guess that's kind of hard for you to understand. . . .

"Anyway, to the point. . . .

"Fuck, I've forgotten what I wanted to say. I called for a particular reason, honest I did. I just can't remember what it is just now. Son of a bitch.

"Sorry if I disturbed you, bud. I feel so fucked up sometimes."

*   *   *

It is after nine AM before Donald can drag himself downstairs, push himself downstairs, a long tepid shower having done nothing to enliven him. He has performed all of his morning ablutions in their natural order, shaving showering brushing combing and dressing as ritualistically as a priest administering extreme unction, yet he feels no less unholy than he did the night before, no more prepared for the glare of another day. His muscles are rubbery but there is no bounce in his step, no spring in his summer.

The kitchen is empty but for Deirdre, who makes it seem emptier still. She is seated at the breakfast nook, sipping coffee, smiling enigmatically. Donald, after the brusque shock of seeing her there, recovers sufficiently for a perfunctory nod of hello, then aims himself toward the counter and their Taiwanese plastic brewmaster, CoffeeSan.

"Somebody doesn't look so hot," Deirdre says, sounding happy.

Donald keeps his back to her, keeps his mouth shut as he fills a mug with coffee.

"Guilty conscience keep you awake?"

Slowly he turns. Sip of coffee, insincere smile. He says, "I dreamed you had triple sixes tatooed on your forehead."

73

Deirdre blanches. Five seconds of abject terror before she gets a grip on herself. "That's nothing to joke about, young man."

And his morning shines a tiny gleam brighter. "Did you know that, according to the most recent *Newsweek* poll, eighty-eight percent of America believes that Jerry Falwell is the antichrist?"

But he has gone too far, he has crossed into the absurd. "So you're not the only moron in this country," she says.

Brief fight, quick defeat. Donald asks, "Where's Jess?"

"It's after nine, where would you expect her to be? She's at the flower shop, earning a living."

He grimaces as if stuck with a pin. "How about Travis?"

"Somewhere outside," she says. "He's been awake since dawn. He said he got up to watch the sunrise. After that he made breakfast for his mother and me, banana waffles. Too bad you couldn't get out of bed. After that he took some garbage bags and said he was going to pick up litter along the streets."

Donald shakes his head in wonder. "What a boy."

"There's something seriously wrong with him, I agree."

74

"He's a little too good maybe. He'll grow out of it."

"Do you know what he told me this morning?"

Something unbelieveable, Donald thinks. Grandma, you're pretty. Grandma, you're sweet.

"He said he doesn't believe in Hell."

I'll make him spend a night at your house, Donald thinks. That'll change his tune.

"He said that everything, *everything*, is a manifestation of 'the spirit.' Even drunks, even murderers. He said there is no such thing as evil."

Has he ever seen you naked? Donald wonders, and smiles at his coffee.

"You know what I blame this on, don't you?"

"Of course," Donald says.

"I blame it on you, Donald. On all those drugs you took when you were in college. You and Jessica both, I warned you but would you listen to me? Marijuana, opium, heroin, LSD—"

"Grass, Deirdre, we smoked a little grass. That's all we ever did."

"You were doped up everytime I saw you. I don't know how either of you managed to graduate."

"The professors were all doped up too."

75

"That doesn't surprise me a bit."

"I always wanted to try LSD," he muses, "but I was afraid of it. I was a chicken hippie."

"You messed up your chromosomes, that's what you did."

"Don't you have some unwed mothers to harass this morning?" he asks. "An abortion clinic to picket?"

"I don't go on duty until noon."

"You protest in shifts?"

"And do *you* have anything productive planned for the day? We can always use another soldier in the war against Satan."

He wants to tell her that he has already been wounded, already bludgeoned and crippled, that he has lost too much blood already, he has no malice to give away. Instead he says, "I have other things to do," and he refills his coffee cup.

"You know, there's a slim possibility," Deirdre says, "I mean it's highly unlikely but it is something to consider. Because there *is* a possibility. . . ."

Donald pauses, his back to her. He waits.

". . .that Travis is demonically possessed."

Donald chuckles so hard on his way to the basement that hot coffee splashes from the cup and sizzles the back of his hand. His first happy pain of the day.

*   *   *

Donald eases his car close to the curb, his foot on the brake. Through the open window he calls to his son, ten yards ahead. Travis grins. "Morning, Dad!" From each hand swings a half-filled green garbage bag.

"What would this neighborhood do without you?" Donald asks.

Travis does not like to be complimented. "Somebody would do it."

"Feel like taking a ride into the city with me?"

Travis gazes up the street, spots a lonely piece of litter far away. "Gee, I would, but. . . ."

"I have to deliver some pictures to an editor. After that I'll take you to lunch, okay?"

"What about these?" Travis asks, and hoists the bags.

Donald shuts off the engine and tosses his son the keys. "Put the bag of recyclables in the trunk," he knows his son's routines nearly as well as he knows his own, "and throw the other bag in the back. There's a dumpster be-hind the 7-11."

He feels a kind of triumph in having gotten his son to accompany him. Now the dilemma of knowing what to say. And for a long time there is only silence between them, although Travis seems comfortable enough with it, he smiles at the scenery, he takes it all in, needing not even the radio to entertain him, no sexually-charged thump and scream to set him at his ease.

"Not much summer left," Donald observes finally. "How long before school starts—a couple of weeks?"

"Seventeen days," Travis says.

"Looking forward to your junior year?"

"Sure."

You look forward to everything, Donald thinks, and that's the problem. How can you look forward to your junior year and at the same time look forward to killing yourself? How can you look forward to living *and* dying?

"I'd think you'd want to make better use of your summer vacation than using it to pick up other people's trash," he says.

Travis merely smiles.

"Why aren't you hanging out with your friends? Skateboarding, chasing girls, shoplifting at the mall?"

"Being alone doesn't bother me, Dad. It's by preference. So don't worry, okay? I like how I spend my time."

Donald is about to argue the wisdom of an

anchoritic life when he remembers suddenly his own youth, the long hours spent alone in the woods, the cultivation of a discipline of silence, of wanting to see but not be seen.

And so he says, "I was the same way, I guess."

"You liked being alone?"

Donald nods. "But I was afraid to admit it to anybody."

"For fear of appearing different."

"I reckon so."

"I like being different," Travis says. "I revel in it."

"You've got a lot to revel in."

"Thanks."

"What troubles me though . . . what worries me . . . is what you think about when you're alone."

"What did you think about?"

Donald tries to remember. "Unlike you, I was not a happy child. I was what my mother called 'overly sensitive.' I cried a lot."

"What about?"

"I never really knew. Sometimes, for no apparent reason, I would be overcome with a terrible sadness, and I would start crying. I used to think it was because I could somehow feel the world's pain, all the suffering and grief.

These days I'd probably be labelled a manic-depressive. Except that I'm never manic."

"I sometimes think I can feel the world's joy. So maybe I'm manic-depressive too. Except that I'm never depressed."

"Together we comprise one fullblown nutcase."

"Manic-depression is very common among artistic individuals, did you know that?"

"Seems a big price to pay for something nobody values anymore."

"I would give you some of my happiness if I could, Dad. I really wish I knew how."

Donald is about to say that he would gladly share some of his condition too when it dawns on him, it hits him hard, no, he would not. He does not want his boy to be sad, not ever. Donald would rather be selfish with his sorrow, hoard it, swallow every drop of poison himself. But then he glances at his son and he sees the concern in Travis's eyes, the sympathy and affection. And Donald realizes sadly, guiltily, regretfully, that he has shared some of his grief already.

* * *

Donald's editor on this assignment appears barely half Donald's age. Donald is watching

80

him now, watching James, yes he certainly looks like a James, like an individual whose mother has called him James, not Jimmy, never Jim—maybe Jamie once: upon his induction into Phi Beta Kappa perhaps—since the moment of his birth.

He has probably been wearing those same clothes since he was born, Donald thinks, the Ralph Lauren chinos and pastel plaid shirt, blue cloth belt with brass buckle, Italian leather moccassins, pink socks. He has probably been shaking his head in this very same way, making similar squeaks of disapproval by sucking air between his tongue and cheeks, since his very first glimpse of the world.

James, with his stylishly-cropped blond head stylishly cocked, intermittently sucks air between his cheeks and tongue, flashing his perfectly bonded teeth, as he leans forward over the desk upon which Donald has spread his contact sheets, page after page of Liliputian photos. Occasionally James examines a particular photo with a magnifying glass. He then leans back and, sucking air, shakes his handsome head.

Donald is not used to an editor such as James. Donald is used to editors grizzled and cynical, smelling of cigar smoke and salami sandwiches, paunchy old men in sweatstained white shirts, mustard stains on the tie. There used to be just such an editor working for *this* magazine, for every magazine, but they are all gone now, retired, all charter fishing in the Sea of Cortez. The world is run by Jameses now, and it is a slick world Donald can not get a grip on.

"If you don't like them, just say so," Donald says finally, knowing how long this dawdling can be protracted, almost eager for rejection.

"It's not that, I do like them," James says. "You have a fine talent, a rare talent, there's no question about that. A superlative eye. An awesome gift."

Donald waits. He counts to twenty. "So?"

"I'm puzzled, Donny. I'm a bit . . . confused."

Donald flinches when called Donny. He is called Donny at times by Jessica, by Wright, but coming from James it offends him. He considers calling him Jimmy in return. Better yet, Jimbo. But he wants more than the kill fee for this assignment. He needs more than the kill fee. Travis is waiting in the anteroom and Donald wants to stroll out there ten minutes from now and say, "How does lobster sound for lunch?", not "Let's go grab a burger."

So Donald says, "What is it that puzzles you, James?"

"I'm trying to remember the exact nature of this assignment."

"Various shots of the city," says Donald. "Capture the flavor of the city. Its ethnic richness."

"Exactly!" James says.

Donald counts to twenty. "So?"

"I just don't feel it from these pictures, Donaldo. I'm sorry, maybe it's me but, they just don't move me."

"Call me Donald," Donald says. "All right, James?"

"Everybody in these pictures looks so *blue* to me. So . . . if you'll pardon the expression . . . down tempo."

"These are hard times," Donald says.

"These are grand times. The best of times!"

"The assignment was to capture the look of the city. Who knows the city better than the people in these pictures?

"They wear this city on their faces."

James is staring into the magnifying glass, his face only inches from the desk. "Are these *street people*?" he asks, aghast. "My god, these *are* street people! Just look at their shoes, their clothes. That sixties-kind of crumpled look."

"You wanted an honest depiction of city life, didn't you? So there it is. Right there in front of you."

"This isn't *my* city, Donnyboy. This isn't the city I see out *my* window. These people aren't *my* friends and colleagues. I sent you out to find *that* city. To show how dynamic and energetic and on the move we are. How relentlessly exciting we are. But these. . . . I can't use these pictures. Not a single one of them. To be honest with you, I'm not very comfortable just having them in the building."

Donald scoops up the contact sheets and slips them into his portfolio case. "You're the editor."

"You want to try again? I can give you until tomorrow."

"I think I'll just cut bait on this one, thanks. You'll send a check for the kill fee, of course."

"Of course."

"I hope it doesn't put too big a dent in your allowance," says Donald as he reaches for the door, a last feeble jab as his knees cave-in and he goes down for the count.

But James is young, he's quick, he lays him out with an uppercut. "What *you* get paid? That's bubblegum money."

Donald wobbles into the anteroom, he wears

a dolorous smile. He prays he will not puke. "How does lobster sound for lunch?" he asks.

* * *

Donald steps onto the sidewalk and stops suddenly as if blinded by the sun. He looks up the street and down, he blinks, such a noisy place, so *fast*, nothing will come into focus.

"Should we pop in on your mother?" he asks, unsure of in which direction lies the flower shop. "Surprise her? Invite her to lunch?"

"You seem tense," Travis says. "Is something wrong?"

"I lost the assignment." Why lie?

Travis lays a hand upon his shoulder. "Sorry, Dad. But I guess it wasn't meant to be."

"Travis," Donald begins, but then stops, gives up, he has no strength for a lecture. He takes a slow deep breath, fills his lungs with carbon monoxide, then puffs out the air, deflates himself, blows the anger away.

"Where do you want to eat?" he asks.

"To tell you the truth, Dad, those waffles I had for breakfast are still with me."

"You're not hungry?" Donald certainly is not. He has no appetite at all.

"Let's get a bag of soft pretzels and a Coke and go sit in the square."

Roebling Square is an acre of cobblestones and water fountains splat in the heart of the city, a resting place named for the man who invented wire cable, who built the Brooklyn Bridge, a park filled with pebble and concrete benches upon which it is impossible to comfortably rest.

Donald and Travis sit side by side on one of these benches, knees touching, a bag of pretzels on Travis's end of the bench, a pretzel in each man's hand, mustard smears on Donald's fingers.

"It's a beautiful day," Travis says softly, hoping to soothe. "Don't you think so?"

"Look straight ahead and tell me what you see."

"I see . . . a couple of ladies, they're both very pretty, and they're eating take-out salads from. . . . I can't read the bags, can you?"

"Look behind them."

"Oh yeah, the way the sun glitters through the fountain spray. The colors in the mist. The gleam of the buildings."

"You don't see that guy in Army fatigues, curled up on that bench over there? The guy with the Pacman beach towel over his face? A towel he probably scrounged from a trash can somewhere? You can see *him* through the mist too, can't you?"

"Yeah, well, I see him now, sure."

"Why is it that he's the first thing I see when I look in that direction, but he's the last thing you see?"

Travis has no answer.

Maybe James is right, Donald thinks. Even snotnoses can be right once in awhile. Maybe my work *is* slipping. Maybe I *have* stopped looking at the world the way I used to. Maybe I've developed tunnel vision. A cataract on my soul.

To test himself, Donald looks to the right. Coming onto the square is a young woman in a tight yellow dress, long thin legs, high heels, a very attractive woman. She is carrying a paperback novel. She sits not far away, begins to read, legs crossed at the knee, face to the sun.

I see her, Donald thinks; but what do I see?

I see a beautiful womangirl who is going to lose her beauty in a very few years. Next week or next month she will meet a handsome young man who works in the same office as she. They will fall in love. They will date for a year and a half. He will give her herpes but she won't care because she loves him and intends to marry him. Then he will get a transfer to another city and he will leave her behind. She will sink into a deep depression, start drinking too much, become promiscuous, nonorgasmic, a man-basher, radical feminist, celibate, a strident old woman.

Or she will find a wonderful husband, have two wonderful children, live in a beautiful home in the suburbs, have a beautiful life, and wake up a week before her thirty-fourth birthday with a lump in her breast.

A cyst on her ovary.

Or her daughter will be molested in preschool.

Or they will all be fantastically healthy but her husband will never get the breaks he deserves and they will live a gray and bitter life of good health together, full of silent complaint.

But that same woman, Donald tells himself, ten years ago, maybe as recently as five, I would have seen her differently then. I would have desired her, would have indulged in the sweet pleasure of a harmless fantasy. A hotel room, the bed warm with afternoon sunlight slanting through the window, a tender hour, the slow touch of flesh, sweet soft kiss of gratitude and goodbye.

Where did my lust go? Donald wonders. Where is my ambition, my expectation, my indulgence of hope?

"What are you thinking about, Dad?"

"I'm thinking," Donald says, and he looks at the young woman and sees nothing but grief, "that I wish I had your eyes."

*　*　*

Donald's car is on the ninth floor of the parking garage. Even the elevator ride, that jerky ascension in a scratched metal box, tires him. He steps out of the elevator and is momentarily lost, which way to the car? But Travis knows, his memory is clear, no scar tissue there. Donald follows; the lobotomized patient going home. He spots his car. It looks dirtier, smaller than he remembers.

Donald unlocks Travis's door, then the driver's side, key pushed into the lock, an ingenious contraption, the cold mechanics of sex, the key as pecker, the pecker as key. Donald wishes it were so, that easy, he wishes he could slip his dick into a welcoming keyhole and thus unlock the door onto a better life, air-conditioned and softly padded, heat and music at his fingertips, a steering wheel responsive to every touch, a steerable life, sound-proofed, with lots of room for luggage.

But alas, it is just a car key, it is just a car. A trope is but a trope. Donald sits behind the steering wheel, leans into it. No snuggery here. He had thought this excursion into the city might do him and Travis some good, spark an epiphany, an understanding, but Donald craves only sanctuary now, the dim silence of his basement, a ghostly pal.

As for Travis, he has not yet climbed into the car. He stands against the low concrete wall, surveying the plummet, the dizzying drop. To Donald he appears to be inclining increasingly forward, the abutment across Travis's hips as he with back held straight inches his upper body further and further beyond the edge, toward, it seems, the angle of decline, that posture whereof his center of gravity will find itself bottomless, will slide off the fulcrum, will reach for the ground.

Donald slides out, stands up. "Don't even think it," he warns.

Travis does not move, does not turn, does not speak. He is in love with the void, the sweet empty inbetween.

Cautiously Donald approaches. He is but a desperate lunge away. Now an arm's length. Now a handspan. He slips two fingers under Travis's belt. Holds on for dear life.

"Stop it," he says, his voice quivering and thin.

Time passes, or stands still, Donald knows not which. Finally the pressure pulling on his fingers relents, Travis's weight returns to the concrete, the grip of his heels. When he looks at his father the expression on Travis's face startles Donald. Donald can describe it only as the dopey flush of ecstasy. The vacuous glaze of rapture.

"But doesn't it intrigue you?" Travis asks, beatific Travis, St. Travis of the Marvin Avenue Garage. "Be honest now. Don't you ever feel it calling?"

To be honest or not to be, that is Donald's question. He would lie if he thought he could do so effectively, if he could come up with a convincing fraud, an eloquent persuasion. But something tells him that he is made of cellophane now, Travis can see straight through him, can spot the twisted viscera of his lies.

"When I was a boy," Donald says, and casts a glance to the distant ground, waits to hear it plop like a pebble down a well, his fingers tightening on Travis's belt, "when I was very young, and older, your age and beyond . . . I remember an urge I used to have sometimes."

Travis waits. He smiles. He knows.

"Whenever I was high," Donald says. "Elevated, I mean. At the top of the ferris wheel, for example. On the rim of the Grand Canyon. Et cetera."

"You had an urge."

"I had an urge, at times like that, to take just one more step. Over the edge."

Travis is nodding. "And it wasn't because you felt sad or depressed, either. In fact, just the opposite."

"Niagara Falls," Donald says, remembering. "Pike's Peak. The World Trade Towers."

"It was . . . beautiful somehow, wasn't it? You knew it would feel so good. The grandness of it all. The vast, unending magnificence. You wanted to enter it, to surrender to it. You wanted to *merge*."

Donald feels his son's hand slip into his. Suddenly the city is all around him. Stink of car fumes, dirty concrete, engines echoing through the oilstained labyrinthe, horns honking, briskly clacking footsteps. Donald faces the ledge again, he looks down. He sees two bodies falling hand in hand, *splatsplat* on the pavement, exploded skulls, guts shimmering like two dropped plates of fettucine calamari.

Donald doubles over the edge, he loses his lunch, half a salty pretzel gone, half a lifetime lost.

* * *

They are driving home, a few silent miles

left to go. Travis, quiet now for twenty minutes, clears his throat.

"Are you glad you and Mom had me?" he
asks.

"I love you more than anything in the
world, son."

"But are you glad you had me?"

"I'm not sure I understand what you mean,"
Donald says, although he surely does.

"My existence causes you pain."

"All love is a burden."

"So are you glad you had me or not? Or
wouldn't you rather be free of that burden?"

"If you would stop thinking about killing
yourself, there would be a lot less burden to
go around."

"I can't help who I am, can I? The way I feel
about the world?"

"I don't know," Donald says.

"So are you glad you had me or aren't you?"

Donald takes a long time to reply. He sprays
the windshield with washer fluid, violently
flushes and swats the sticky bug parts away.

"I remember a time when you were little,"
he says. "About three years old, I think. You
were so excited, you came running down to
the basement to show me a picture you had
drawn. It was a picture, you said, of Dorothy

93

and Toto. You laid it in front of me, and then, very excitedly, you started pointing. 'Here are the Munchkins,' you said. 'And here's Glinda. And here's the wicked witch. Here's her dead sister and the house that fell on her and here's the ruby slippers that Dorothy gets. Here's Emerald City and this is the Scarecrow and here's Tin Man and the Cowardly Lion and the Wizard and the flying monkies and here's where *we* live and this is Disneyworld and over here is Mickey Mouse giving Cinderella a great big kiss!'"

"That must have been some picture," Travis says.

"Except for a scribble or two and a couple of crayon smears, it was blank. Which prompted me to say something like, 'Gee, honey, it's a really nice picture, but I'm afraid I don't see any of those people in it.' You flashed me a very disapproving look, and then you said, I'll never forget, you were only three years old, and you said, 'Daddy, you should learn how to use your imagination more.'"

Travis considers the clouds. "And you think that's what I'm still doing, don't you?" he asks. "Imagining beauty where it doesn't really exist."

Donald snaps on the turn signal, his foot taps the brake. "We're home," he says.

* * *

Wright's house after dinner, the picture of rosy suburban calm. A sunset wash of cinnamon light gives the white frame house a radiance, the pink of perfect health. Donald stands across the street, he stares at the silent door. He has nothing to say to the terrible darkness inside that house, no words as quick as flame, no tongue of incandescence to flap from room to room. And yet he knows he must speak, if only to admit there is nothing to say.

Across the street then, the sidewalk. Heavy feet on wooden porch. Where has the sense of familiarity gone?

Donald's finger depresses the bell button. He hears the mechanical ding, it sounds like a bullet shot within a metal barn, two dull ricochets before the slug buries itself in something soft. Donald feels a pair of eyes peering out, he turns quickly to the nearest window, the curtains are drawn, blank, no glimmer of light.

"Wright!" he calls, and jabs the button three crisp times. "Open up, man. Enough of this nonsense!"

He rings again, he knocks, he calls, he raps his knuckles sore. And after each attempt he pauses, listens, the silence inside the house sounds even more profound for his interruption, the neighborhood a lumen less bright, as if the house is expanding imperceptibly, absorbing illumination and turning it inside out, a two-story black hole, seven rooms of gravity.

Donald sinks to his haunches, then drops to his knees. With one finger he pushes open the mail slot, puts his eyes to the narrow slit. He sees a strip of hallway, a turn of stairs. Everything appears normal, and is all the more horrifying for that.

Donald draws away, closes his eyes, lets the mail slot flap shut. There is no air to breathe, he feels faint. The door when he looks is still there, the mail slot no mirage.

Again his finger pushes open the tiny hinged door, but this time he puts his mouth to the opening. He feels the same enormous tenderness and despair as when he puts his mouth to Jessica, his finger inside her too, the same need, the same confidence of blundering.

"Wright?" he asks, softly now, his voice strange and high, muted to his ears. "Buddy? Come and let me in, okay?"

But there are no footsteps padding toward him. No chuckle of concession.

"Jesus, Wright. I wish I knew what to say about this. I wish . . . I wish I could *do* something."

It all sounds so foolish, inarticulate, inept. Only sincerity gives the words any lift at all, keeps them from plopping on the other side of the door, as silent as dirt.

"I just want to be with you, pardner. I just want to see you again. I just want to be able to tell you . . . face to face . . . that there's never been a better friend than you. That I'm better for having had you as a friend. And that I . . . you. . . .

"Goddamn it, Wright, come and open this fucking door!"

And Donald trudges home unanswered through the gray thick weight of dusk, his heart as battered as his knuckles.

* * *

Jessica wants to make love.

Donald is reluctant because he knows the futility of it, the unavailing promise. What after all does this nonprocreative sex accomplish? It frenzies the hormones into hope, pumps deceitful endorphins into the brain, tucks the warm cozy of wellbeing around tingling flesh only to draw it away, leave you naked and sad.

Donald would rather brood than make love, he would rather hug his pessimism. But he loves his wife and knows how easily she

97

bruises. She will interpret his lack of desire for her as a lack of desire for her, and that is not the case at all, he desires her with all his heart, he wants, if the truth be known, to make tender healing love to every woman in the world, to grasp the hand of every fellowman, tousle every child's hair, scratch the belly of every dog, feed crackers to every squirrel. And because he can not do it all, what good is a token gesture?

Even so, Jessica's hand is warm. She pulls lovingly on his cock, introduces it to the soft cheek of her moist inner thigh. Oh yes it does feel good, there is no denying the appeal of this simmering slippery rhythm, her breasts flattened against his hollow chest, her teeth grazing his ticklish neck.

And for awhile her ardency thaws him, the familiar grip of familiar flesh, the soothing slurp of repetition. Everything will be okay, he thinks. Everything will work out fine. Even the growing urgency revivifies. He works harder now, gaining energy rather than expending it. He knows the pattern of her breath and the language of her muscles and he attunes all movement to Jessica's pleasure, her pleasure is his joy, oh my wife, my cherished one, oh my soul forgive such black neglect, sweet god erase my sins, why don't we do this more often?

The afterglow is warm. But heat rises, evanescing. This crucible does not obtain. A scent of ash fills his nostrils, he smells himself, tastes dessication. His only hope now, remote, is to avoid this crematory stench in sleep.

Jessica wants to talk. "So tell me," she says. "Anything interesting happen between you and Travis today?"

A lunar bleakness descends upon him, a dusty craterlike sorrow. "We had a fine time together," he says. "It was a nice afternoon."

"Did you talk about . . . you know."

"Indirectly," he says.

"And?"

"I think he's coming around."

"Really?" says Jessica, and hugs him tightly, the fraud. "Thank god."

"Pleasant dreams," he tells her, and begins to turn, but she holds fast to his arm, her head glued to his chest.

"How'd things go with the magazine?"

A moment's thought. Surrender. "I lost the assignment."

This she had not expected, she never expects him to fail. A delicate kiss upon the sweaty cleavage of his arm. "I'm sorry, sweetie."

"I'm the one who's sorry," says he, and basks in the momentary heat of self-pity, its sputtering flame.

"Don't worry. There'll be lots of other assignments. Lots of other jobs."

"Right," he says. "There's a fortune to be made in kill fees."

And he pulls away, disconnecting as tenderly as selfish despair will allow. He stares at the wall, black, because it is prettier than what dances on the back of his eyelids, that rainbow of fears, that Hieronymus Bosch landscape of inexpressible words, unattainable acts, meaningless gestures and infertile thoughts.

Jessica caresses a shoulder, she kisses his spine. Then, "Oh, I forgot. When you were out walking tonight, after dinner, your phone rang down in the basement."

"Okay," he says. He sucks in a dusty draft of air, his body pneumatic, his joints needing pressure to work. Tired legs fall over the side of the bed.

"It can wait until morning, can't it?" Jessica asks.

"I'm sure it can," he says, but continues forward, an object in motion. In the darkness he pulls on only his undershorts, no robe could keep him warm.

* * *

"Big news, Don."

Wright's voice is tremulous and hushed, a teenager's voice breathless with secret.

"I had a wet dream just now. I just now woke up from it, my pants are still wet. Can you believe it?

"I mean Christ, I haven't been able to get a hard-on for close to a year now. And just ten minutes ago I came in my pants!"

Donald is short of breath suddenly, gasping as he leans over the answering machine, hands gripping the cold stiff knobs of his knees. His toes feel as if they are soaking in a pan of ice water, a heavy lump of frozen lead shivers in his chest, his hair stands taut with a ferocious itch.

"I fucked the Big Blonde, Donny. I fucked her good. She came too, same time I did.

"Man oh man, it was something, pardner. It was something else, Don. Something else entirely. . . ."

Wright is sobbing now, breathing thickly, throat sticky with phlegm. He is muttering but in a voice too dim, muffled, as if he has turned his head away, is speaking into his pillow. Donald strains to hear, he lays an ear to the speaker grate. His own tears slide into the mechanism, they flavor his lips, tickle his nose. Wright continues for thirty seconds more, muttering to somebody else, to himself, and then returns to the phone, holds it to his mouth, a warm deep breath, a shiver, a pause, he speaks.

"I heard you pounding on my door not long ago. I almost came down and let you in too, I almost did. I'm glad I didn't, though. Because after you left I took a nap. And that's when it happened with me and the Big Blonde. Happened like . . . nothing I ever would have imagined. . . .

"Anyway, bud, listen. The real reason I called is, you're going to be getting a package one of these days." A soft chuckle. "A *big* package.

"You'll know what to do with it. I'm not worried at all."

Another pause, as sharp as a wound.

"Anyway, friend. . . ."

And the final pause has no end. Donald waits, holding his breath, straining to catch a muttered word, a question, explanation, any small utterance of illumination, a spark, explosion, any news of life will do.

So he waits. He waits. Wright's telephone receiver dully clicks, the connection severed, end of transmission. Yet still Donald remains bent double and all but naked over his answering machine. Yet still he waits. Yet still he listens. He has lost all capacity but fear, he has forgotten how to stand and move, how to find his way upstairs.

*   *   *

"Fuck off."

"Jerry, please. I need to talk to somebody."

"It ain't me, babe."

"But you heard that message on my machine, didn't you? Wright's lost it, he's gone over the edge."

"End of vacation, old pal. Time to go home."

"Wait! Wait! There's something I need to ask."

Silence.

"Jerry? Are you still here? Where'd you go, Jer?"

The strip of negatives hanging from the wire seems to have moved somehow, shifted, turned away from the light. The negatives are stiff, curled up from the bottom, curled inward from the sides; aged, it seems to Donald, as they were not aged before. In any case their position has changed so that the red bulb shining above the worktable no longer shines through the parasailing Jerry, casts no image

103

now, no garrulous shadow on the wall. Donald maneuvers and turns and pulls the strip, he twists and stretches, but he can not convince it to catch the light.

Donald frees the entire strip from the thin wire. The negatives are surprisingly brittle, a snakeskin of younger days. With his left hand he holds the transparent image of Jerry close to the red bulb, and, facing the opposite wall, he searches it for an adumbration, a teasing friendly figure. There, ha! a flicker of smile.

"Jer? Come on, buddy, I know you're here. Quit playing games."

And there, yes, for just an instant, Jerry's grinning face, a wink. But then on the wall there is a sudden smear of brightness—Donald has touched the negatives to the bulb, they flare and burn, they sizzle like a fuse.

Donald tosses the flaming strip to the floor, he stomps the fire out, he sears his naked heel. A portion of the strip remains stuck to the bulb, celluloid bacon, soon only bacon fat, a smoking splotch of grease.

And as Donald watches, amazed, aghast, the bulb pops. The tiny red sun explodes, a brief blinding fulmination. Donald ducks, covers his face. Splinters of glass, a sharp tinkling rain. He stands huddled in darkness, cowering, knock-kneed, shivering in a primitive naked stance, this superstitious man, this witness to the Little Bang, the unsupernova, this man who wonders, too afraid to look, if the world he walked his path upon is gone.

*   *   *

Donald is sitting on his basement sofa and thinking that this is the sad truth, a man's habits avail nothing, routine does not insure nor custom protect. Order exists only in the single captured moment, the photograph, a snapshot of order past. Yet even here there is no permanence. Even in the captured moment transcience reigns. Photographs change from instant to instant, from eye to eye. The circle of confusion, just a tiny white spot on the film when the photo is taken, caused by flaw of light or aberrance of lens, is imperceptible on the virgin print, a freckle unnoticed, a single impure dot; but look at the photo a day later, a week, and the circle of confusion has grown, a gauzy halo now, now a moon and now the sky itself and now the foreground too is engulfed and the subject blurred, who took this shot? what day was this? where has all life's clarity gone?

Donald gazes a moment longer at the awkward manuscript of his and Wright's unpublished book. He flips through the final thick

pages, his photos on the right, Wright's sentimental verses on the left. He does not remember taking these photos so much as he
remembers Wright's excitement, Wright fairly
skipping through the woods, a clumsy baggy-
trousered man exuberant with hope, not losing
his pagan ecstasy even when he trips on a root,
slams into the soft dirt, recovers his glasses
and squinting through the smudge of humus
cries, "Donny! Donny! Look at this skunk cab-
bage, my god it's exquisite! Take a picture, take
a picture, I can write a sonnet about this!"

Donald, from the very beginning, is never
optimistic about the project. He knows it will
not sell. Who wants to look at tree moss, or to
read the accompanying ode? More to the
point, who will pay thirty, forty, fifty dollars
for the privilege? No, Donald goes along with
the plan only for the joy of those days, for
Wright's undiluted joy and Donald's own, a
less intoxicating joy, a lighter brandy instilled
with melancholy, spritzed with wist.

And now Donald lays the book away. A peculiar virus of fatigue has infected him. His
muscles are as mud, his bones dead twigs, and
yet his mind is racing, turbid with a thousand
shrieking germs of thought. He can not risk
lying down now, doing nothing, closing his

eyes, he will surely go mad. And this house he loves feels shrunken and as heavy as serge tonight; it chokes and makes him itch.

From the hamper in the laundry room he recovers some clothes, a pair of jeans, pungent sweatshirt, dirty socks. His sneakers he finds in the living room, under the coffee table. He needs air and movement now, he needs space and anonymity. He feels the urge to scream.

Donald tiptoes into the kitchen, toward the back door. A glance at the clock: 12:49 AM. He is into a new day now, stealing into it, smelling of days before.

On the rear patio he pulls the door softly closed, hears the lock click shut. Halfway through the yard he trips over the lawn sprinkler, slams onto the soft ground, loses his glasses, fumbles in the grass. He finds his glasses finally and puts them on. Grass clippings stuck to the lenses. The blur of condensation. *Donny! Donny!* he hears. *Get a picture of that, it's exquisite!*

And he lies there motionless for ten long minutes, weeping tiny moons of melting light, inhaling the cutgrass sweetness of all his unraked yesterdays.

* * *

Donald has been walking, walking, up one street and down another, avoiding when he can the light, pausing from time to time to gaze upon a house darkened but for the spectral blue flicker of a TV set playing behind the curtain. What is life like in there, he wonders, inside that house? What fears keep *that* individual awake so late?

And Donald tries to picture it: an overweight man, beer gut straining at his tee-shirt, watching without interest Hope and Crosby and Dorothy Lamour. This man, who has never had the luck he deserves, still just a foreman on the loading dock, has long ago stopped flagellating himself with regret and no longer bothers to voice his remorse, those mistakes carved indelibly in the homely granite of his life. He smiles at Bob Hope's ball-eyed naivete, a tired smile, wanting to be amused. Bing faces the camera, skinny basset-hound face, who could argue with a face like that? "You should have stayed in college, boy," Bing tells him. "You should have done like your brother." And Dorothy Lamour joins in. "You shouldn't have settled for Marge. You think she's taking jazzercise three times a week for a slob like you?"

Donald wants to go to the front door and ring the bell. "Hiya pal," he would say, and clap the stranger warmly on the shoulder. "Slip on some shoes and let's take a stroll."

At the next house they invite the aging widow to come along, to walk between them, wherever they are going. Forget for just a moment that blue-eyed jarhead whose dogtags still dangle between your withered breasts. Give grief some air.

And at the next house, and the next. You're welcome to join us, we are all friends here.

They are zombies of a kind, but harmless, not a cannibal among them. Any living dead in this house? Any misery here?

Up one night street and down another they march, the street swollen with solemn bodies, there is no need to chat, to inquire or confess. They know the value of commiseration.

Donald takes the point, he is the drum major of despair. He feels the ranks behind him ever-growing. People filing from each building passed, each life a novel of misfortune, of accidents and errors, opportunities missed, dreams lost, faith as diffuse as the smog.

Their faith is in Donald now. He seems to know where he is going. He doesn't know but that is all right too, they have all been nowhere up till now, at least they are moving, their bodies if not their lives are in motion.

And at long last the procession crests a low asphalt rise. The street joins the highway here, and below them runs the river, a two-lane bridge. The river is black but spreckled with starlight, a streak of yellow moonglow shimmers like an eel. *The river,* Donald thinks. A liquid demarcation, gurgling vein, coursing jugular of the sleeping land.

"To the river!" he cries, and waves his forces onward, commander of the night.

There is not a soul behind him but Donald does not look back. To him the summer darkness is all but billowing with woe.

*   *   *

Black water curling around concrete pilings. Unresisting water, lazy splashes, sluggardly flow. It is old water above which Donald stands, water wise with mud and pithy with submerged debris. How far down? he wonders, and tries to gauge the distance in the dark. Twenty feet? Twenty-five?

The teeth of the bridge's gridwork nibble at his soles, bite into his feet, so long has he been standing here. The brindled rail hard across his hips, gripped with both hands as as if to hold the bridge in place. He is leaning out, out, a near right angle of flagging flesh.

110

Dim yellow lights mark each end of the bridge but there is no light here in the middle where Donald stands. He feels invisible, impervious to the fleeting sweep of an occasional headlight. A car passes and the bridge rattles beneath him, it shudders, creaks, and then quiets quickly, embarrassed to have made a noise, ashamed of its weakness, the stress of metal fatigue.

There is a feeling like a hook in Donald's mouth, a sharptipped tugging on his cheek. He works up a bomb of spit and lets it fall. It disappears almost instantly. He listens for the splash but hears not even that.

Where does this river go? he wanders. Where would it carry a man who does not resist? It flows south, he knows that at least. Into the Ohio, the Mississippi, the Gulf of Mexico, the Atlantic Ocean. Past Epcot Center and the Magic Kingdom. A slow meander through the cays of Florida, past Sloppy Joe's Bar, shrimp and egrets. Then out into the Gulf Stream, bye bye Bahamas, strains of the Spoleto Festival, picking up speed now, streamlined by the current into a deadhead torpedo, hello Cape Hatteras, so long Philadelphia, through the garbage sludge of wretched and teeming shores, past L. L. Bean's, the Grand Banks, as slim as an arrow

111

now, a last shaft of bone, tugged left by the gravity of Newfoundland, slingshotting home, making barely a buzz as he is wave-tossed ashore and comes to rest in Greenland, a splinter in the spume of Cape Farewell, ice-crusted, buried, becoming tundra.

* * *

Donald hears the footsteps approaching, just three soft scrapes before they stop. Still bent far out over the railing but with his head even lower now, the blood having filled his face so that his eyes seem to bulge and his mouth to gape and he thinks *I am a flounder,* he freezes now, waits, not even daring to turn his head to discover Is it a policeman? A pervert? A ghostly soldier from his AWOL troop?

"Dad?" the someone says.

A familiar word but the voice is strange, the pitch elevated, the inflection sounds like taffy stretched too far.

Donald's head lifts slightly and slowly turns. Travis stands a mere four feet away, skinny arms hugging a skinny chest.

"Are you sick?" he asks.

Maybe it is because of the whoosh of blood in Donald's ears, but everything sounds peculiar now, muffled, under several feet of water.

He pushes himself erect, it is harder to do than he would have thought. He wipes a dribble of saliva from the corner of his mouth.

"What?" he says.

"You looked like you were . . . throwing up again."

He has never seen Travis quite like this before. The boy appears terrified, as timid as a rabbit.

"I'm okay," Donald says.

"Well then . . . what were you doing like that? What are you doing out here?"

Donald has a sensation of water draining from his ears, of sound becoming less fluid. Yet still he is disoriented by this sudden appearance of one so unexpected. He glances at the water below, a silver leaf of starlight. What *am* I doing here? he wonders. He doesn't know if he knows or not. He doesn't know if he wants to know.

He turns to Travis again, who is now more tangible than ever, less silhouette and more boy, flesh of Donald's flesh, he sees himself in those eyes. "What are *you* doing here?" he asks, but gently, and with a smile. "Does your mother know you're out wandering around so late at night?"

Travis shakes his head no. "I was sitting up at

my window when you left the house," he says. "I saw you fall in the yard, and I thought maybe you got hurt, you took so long to get up. . . ."

"Why were you still awake at midnight?"

Travis considers his feet. "You just lay there in the yard for so long, I finally pulled on my pants and came downstairs. But just as I got to the door, you stood up."

"And you've been following me ever since," says Donald. "Why didn't you call out to me? We could have walked together."

"It seemed to me," Travis says, and his words have the weight of confession, "that you probably didn't want any company. That you probably weren't just, you know, taking a walk."

"So why did you decide to stop following me just a minute ago?"

Travis says nothing. He is staring so softly at his father, it breaks Donald's heart. Donald can see a yellow shine of moonlight in his eyes.

"Can we just go home now?" Travis asks. He sniffs, and is shivering, but to Donald there has never been a night so warm.

"Let's go," Donald says, and they walk across the gridwork side by side, Donald's shoulder rubbing Travis's arm. Donald notices however that despite the difference in their height they walk stride for stride, paces perfectly matched. And he wonders who has fit his stride to whose.

They are nearly halfway home before either one speaks.

"Dad?" Travis says, and Donald says "Hmmm?"

"Please don't ever do that again."

"I wasn't doing anything," Donald tells him, and walks, and a few moments later he promises, "I won't."

* * *

The postman, whose name is Phil, a young man not yet thirty in his blue walking shorts and knee socks, his summer uniform, steps onto Wright's porch at approximately 9:20 AM, intending to push Wright's mail through the mail slot, a department store circular, a postcard offering Wright two weeks' first class accomodations in Bermuda if he calls the toll-free number within twenty-four hours, and a bill from his urologist. But the door is standing open a crack and there is a note taped to the mail slot: *Please come upstairs, Phil. Thank you.*

Phil goes upstairs, but cautiously. Wright is after all a middle-aged bachelor, and an English teacher to boot. A suspicous combination. Phil has never considered having a homosexual relationship but the life of a civil servant hasn't been all it's cracked up to be. In four years of faithful service he has not yet been seduced by a gorgeous neglected housewife or a sex-crazed teenaged cheerleader home alone. On second thought maybe Wright has a woman up there and they want Phil for one of those ménage things. Maybe Wright has *two* women up there and it's more than an old guy like him can handle.

Phil's erection by the time he reaches the second floor landing is flicking as Benny Goodman's clarinet must have slowly flicked when playing "Exactly Like You," the bluesy strains of which now spiral out softly from the bedroom on the right. Phil wonders if he should enter with his pants down, show from the start that he is a man of the world. But he decides finally to play it nonchalant. He hangs his mailbag on the bannister post and saunters toward the bedroom with what he hopes is an unsuspecting smile on his lips.

Wright is lying peacefully on his bed, lying on his back with his left hand atop his chest, right hand at his side, his eyes are closed, his skin pale blue, he is wearing a tuxedo. *Memories from the Days of Swing* plays nonstop on an obsolete 8-track tape player on the nightstand.

Wright wears what appears to be an unsuspecting smile on his lips.

Phil attempts mouth-to-mouth resuscitation but Wright's jaw is as stiff as an unoiled hinge. Phil rips Wright's shirt open, spraying mother-of-pearl buttons, and then hammers on Wright's chest.

When it dawns on Phil suddenly that this setup smacks of suicide, that Wright is long past resurrection, that he, Phil, has done considerable disarray to a perfectly presentable corpse, Phil hies his ass downstairs but quick. He stands gasping on the top porch step until he gets his breath under control, until the bombing run stops booming in his ears.

In the kitchen then, the sunniest room, he dials 9-1-1. He returns to the porch, where he waits for the authorities to arrive.

Donald hears this story in various places and versions from various sources over the next few days. He hears it from Phil, from Deirdre, from the night clerk at 7-11. He feels cheated by Phil, who—in self-defense probably, not maliciously, Donald will grant him that—has turned the entire episode into a joke. Donald feels cheated that *he* was not summoned to discover the body. That Wright chose to take leave of him without even that consid-

117

eration. Without as much as a *See you around, bud.* The courtesy of a simple *Goodbye.*

*   *   *

Jessica is furious because Donald did not tell her that Wright was dying. She seems to blame the death on Donald's silence, as if friendship were a dark conspiracy, an evil pact. Donald feels the same way. He always will.

"He didn't want anybody to know, Jess. He didn't want *me* to know. I felt compelled to honor his wishes."

"Bullshit," she says. She has been angry for three days now, still angry on this crystal morning as she dresses for the funeral, as she over-blushes her cheeks while sitting at the dressing table, Donald hangdog in his wrinkled blue suit sitting perched on the edge of their unmade bed.

"What about surgery?" she demands. "Chemotherapy? Cobalt treatments? Plutonium?"

"Plutonium, uranium, explodium, even kryptonite, it wouldn't have made a difference. The chain reaction had already begun. The meltdown couldn't be stopped."

"Don't even talk to me," she says.

118

He understands her anger, which is a mask for something else, so many things.

"Should we take Travis?" he wonders.

Her mascara wand poises in mid-air, eyes close to the glass, searching their own reflection.

"It might help," Donald says. "On the other hand, it might hurt."

Jessica, like him, does not know.

Donald stands finally, he goes to Travis's room. Travis is not there. So be it, Donald thinks, the decision made.

He waits downstairs until Jessica descends. She is wearing too much blush but he says not a word. Her eyes are as red as her cheeks. Silently they walk outside to the car. Travis is seated in the back, white shirt and tie, no jacket.

"I'm going along," he says.

Donald nods, slides in behind the steering wheel, starts the engine. Jessica turns to address her son. "No sport jacket?" she says.

"The arms are too short."

"We can get you a new one on Monday."

* * *

Jessica says, "It was a nice funeral, wasn't it?"

119

"It was horrible," says Donald. "Every funeral is horrible, no matter how nice it is."

And Travis stares out the car window, his gaze scours the sky.

* * *

The funeral is over, the dead interred, the wounded still wandering the earth. A brown panel truck is parked in Donald's driveway as he returns with wife and son. A brown-uniformed man is pushing a dolly loaded with three cardboard boxes toward Donald's front porch. There are eight boxes stacked on the porch already.

"What's all this?" Donald asks.

"I waited a half hour and then I started unloading," the delivery man says. "Wait here, I got an invoice for you to sign."

Donald kneels on the porch and rips open one of the boxes. The first thing he sees is Wright's smiling face, his own grinning glossily beside it, a black and white photo, 11″ × 14″, of Wright and Donald standing arm-in-arm knee-deep in clover, a photo Donald himself shot. There are forty-nine more photos all the same in this same box, forty-nine more book jackets, forty-nine more copies of *A Nature Walk*.

The delivery man hands Donald the form to

sign, he brings another load of books. When he finishes wheeling the dolly back and forth there are twenty cardboard boxes on the porch, fifty books inside each box.

"Here you go," the delivery man says, "the very first copy." And he places in Donald's hand a single book photoside up. Scrawled in black ink across the sky of the picture is *To Donald, good friend. The one I could always count on. Hang tough, buddy. Wright.*

Donald is surrounded by boxes, boxed in by boxes, hunkered down low in a bunker of boxes.

Jessica says, "It must have cost him a fortune."

And Travis asks, "What are you going to do with them all, Dad?"

And the delivery man drives away. "Enjoy!"

* * *

Another sleepless night.

In his basement office Donald sits as still as a ceramic dog in the center of his unsupporting sofa. Everywhere he looks stands a cardboard box, enough to deflect a mortar attack. And yet he feels disarmed by them, blasted naked despite the heavy gray sweatsuit he wears. His answering machine is silent, his

darkroom nothing but dark. What is he supposed to do with all these books? Wright, you
goof, what the hell am I supposed to do?

He can feel the weight of all those books just
as surely as if each were stacked upon his shoulder. He wonders if the floor might collapse, a
hole punched into the earth, down he is
dragged with a thousand dud bombs tumbling
about his head, pages riffling, useless flapping
wings, down through the thin dust of anthro-
pology, the crust of theology, geology after geology whupping by, no more chronology,
goodbye etiology, etymology, parapsychology.

This would be fine, he thinks, if he could
count on plopping into a molten core. A quick
sizzle and he is nothing but steam, as are the
books, his worries all behind him.

But no, it could never happen so sweetly. He
would crash through the underside of existence and just keep falling, falling even though
there is nowhere to go, there is nothing here
but gravity, the only absolute. . . .

Donald hears a creak on the stairs. He turns.
That naked foot, size eleven, can be none but
Travis's. Those long skinny legs in short-pant
pajamas, it tugs at Donald's heart.

"Okay if I come down?" Travis asks.

"Sure. What's up?"

Travis does not answer yet but instead concentrates on climbing over a low stack of books, a lanky hurdler in slow motion. He eases down on the edge of the sofa cushion, knees sticking up nearly as high as his chin.

"Can't sleep?" Donald asks.

Travis shrugs. He reaches forward and lifts off the coffee table the signed copy of *A Nature Walk*. He turns it over to the photo, his father and Wright's dopey smile.

"You lost another friend," Travis says.

And Donald says, "Yup." He would say more, start a conversation, chat, if only he remembered how. But he has gone crashing through the earth and left even semeiology behind.

"You know who I was thinking about tonight?" Travis asks. "Uncle Jerry. Remember him?"

"Sure," Donald says.

"He died, what . . . four or five years ago?"

"Seems more like yesterday."

"Do you still think about him, Dad?"

"A lot."

"You miss him, don't you?"

"A lot."

Travis nods. "I remember what a nice guy he was. He called me Mr. T, remember?"

"T for Travis, yep."

They nod silently; bookends. A few moments later Travis opens the book at random.

123

The photo is of a large wild mushroom, poisonous, the top concave, fluted edges turned up, a bright orange chalice holding a shimmer of wet sunshine.

"This is beautiful," Travis says.

Donald is about to say thank you, those close-up shots are tricky in such meager light, when Travis continues. "He wrote this, didn't he?"

"Hmmm?" Donald says.

"Your friend Wright. He wrote this beautiful poem.

"'So deadly to consume,'" Travis reads, "'so filling to behold, The beauty of its bitter taste can warm the chillest cold.'"

Donald asks, "You like that?"

"It's beautiful."

"It's not very good poetry."

"I don't care. I like what it says."

He closes the book, holds it on his lap, his fingers on his father's glossy face. "You remember the other night?" Travis asks. "When I followed you down to the river? I never told you why I was still awake when you left the house."

"No, you never did."

"I had a dream about Uncle Jerry that night."

"Oh?"

"Just a piece of a dream, I guess. I hardly remember any of it."

Donald waits.

"All I can remember is . . . I dreamed I saw him standing there beside my bed. Just for a second or two. And then I woke up. That's why I was sitting by the window when you went outside."

"So," Donald says.

Travis flips the book over, looks at the front cover. He places the book on the coffee table. "You wouldn't let me go to Uncle Jerry's funeral," he says. "I remember that."

"He wasn't your real uncle, you know."

This is an insufficient explanation, no answer at all, as Donald soon learns from Travis's silence.

"We thought you were too young," Donald says. "That it wasn't a good idea. That . . . you know . . . you were too young."

Still Travis says nothing. Donald wonders what the boy is thinking. Feeling. How to get at and hold the sweet truth of this child.

"So that's why you insisted on going to Wright's funeral," Donald says.

Travis's answer, as he continues to stare at *A Nature Walk*, is a noncommital shrug.

"I'm sorry if I was wrong," Donald says. "In not letting you go to Jerry's."

"I don't know," says the boy a long moment

125

later. "I'm beginning to think that all of us, no matter how old we get to be, are still too young for that kind of thing."

And Donald sleeps that night in restful marvel of the adolescent mind, its elasticity and spaciousness, as nimble as a springbok, as vast and forgiving as the Serengeti Plain.

* * *

It is a Sunday afternoon in late September, a drive in the country, a new family routine. Travis is at the wheel, his mother beside him, Donald sprawled in the rear with his hand steadying a short stack of books. Here is what they are doing, what they have done for the past five Sundays, what they will do for the next three hundred and twenty-eight:

Each is responsible each Sunday for three copies of *A Nature Walk*. Donald began with the obvious choices, he left one copy in the bus station, one in a restaurant, one in a filling station restroom. But he is learning from his companions to be more creative now, to keep his eyes open, look for harder possibilities.

Jessica, for example, spots an austere white farmhouse down a long narrow lane. With a single glance she takes in the hungry fields of corn, the milkbarn, cows, the neat garden and quiet yard, long hours of toil, vast winter nights. She places a copy of the book in the mailbox at the end of the lane, she raises the flag. "Onward," she says.

Travis pulls over next to a low concrete bridge abutment. Gazing down into the shallow dirty stream is a girl approximately Travis's age, a plain girl in a too-long dress, a gawky girl whom Travis knows immediately, this stranger, he knows how she sits at her desk at school and seldom speaks, never raises her hand, no parties for this girl, no dances, just dreams. So Travis pulls along beside her, he winds down the window. "Excuse me," he says, and when she turns hesitantly, afraid to be spoken to, he hands her a book, "This is for you," he says. She looks at it curiously, with effort returns his smile. "What for?" she asks, and Travis says, "You'll see."

Donald loves these slow afternoons, the healing air, incense of dirt and grass and trees, music of crows, salubrious light. He holds his camera on his lap, he captures moments, he lets them go.

Sometimes, through long stretches of un-peopled land, Jessica opens the book and reads aloud. They are learning to laugh with Wright's insistent lines. *Asparagus,* wrote Wright, *please bear with us.*

Donald sometimes confesses his hope for an

international assignment, of trips to Belgrade, Moscow, Beijing, Panama City, a trunkful of Wright's books in tow, Jessica and Travis and maybe even Deirdre to help him dispense them throughout ingenuous lands.

They talk of the scenery, of possibilities, of re-modeling that needs to be done, of temporary and transient things. It is all very important to Donald. It is a ritual as important to him as what they do not say aloud, what they never once dis-cuss, this house of mirrors, this two-headed cow, this babble, this silence, this danse ma-crabe, this Irish wake, this graduation day, this morning after, this night before, this insult, this tease, this tohubohu, this argument, this agree-ment, this funeral march, this wedding, this foreplay, this failure, this pearl in the mud, this wink, this sneer, this nightmare, this dream, this lump in the throat and this pang in the heart, this captured moment, this speeding comet, this trumpet blast, this cotton in the ears, this poisonous mushroom, this cool drop of dew, this insatiable hunger, this Sunday so alive. . . .